# The Journey to Jaffna

by Rajes Bala

The Conrad Press

*Journey to Jaffna*
Published by The Conrad Press in the United Kingdom 2024
Tel: +44(0)1227 472 874
www.theconradpress.com
info@theconradpress.com
ISBN 978-1-916966-37-6
Copyright ©Rajes Bala 2024
All rights reserved.
Typesetting and Cover Design by: Levellers
The Conrad Press logo was designed by Maria Priestley.
Printed and bound in Great Britain by Clays Ltd, Elcograf S.p.A.

Please note: Rajes Bala is Rajeswary Balasubramaniam

# Chapter 1

(Christmas Eve, December 1977 - London)

Param felt anxious and couldn't sleep. He turned from left to right often and tried to doze off again, but he was too restless to settle and relax. He was about to visit his family in Sri Lanka whom he hadn't seen nearly twelve years. The reason for this eventuality was sleeping on the bed next him.

Param had married Mary without his father's approval, not the done thing for a traditional Hindu Tamil man from Jaffna.

Mary instinctively stretched her hand across his chest, as if trying to calm him out of his irritability and anxiety, as she had done since the day they'd met at university in London.

Param was just over twenty-three years old, a postgraduate student. He was far from home in a strange place, trying to figure out the people and the atmosphere. When he and Mary had met at the student canteen she looked as nervous as him, sitting at the next table. Param wanted to tell her, I was like you, too, when I was twenty years old on my first day at Colombo University, as he thought she was a first-year student.

Mary was a beautiful young girl with long blonde hair and a loving sincere smile, and her expression was courteous. He thought she was just twenty years old or less, a new student, nervous as he was at the university in a foreign place.

He said, 'hello' to her in a soft low tone. He knew she noticed his nervousness, too.

She said, 'hello', and after a pause she asked where he was from.

He said, 'far away from London, I am from Ceylon.' He could tell by the way she raised her eyebrows with an understanding expression that she felt a bit sorry for him to far away from home.

'I am from Dorset, like you, I am new to London.'

They were quiet for a minute or so. She wanted to continue the conversation and be welcoming to him in this new place, 'I read the island of Sri Lanka is beautiful, and the people are friendly,' she said in a jolly rhythm.

He smiled and nodded and wanted to tell her, 'Yes, it is'.

Suddenly he felt so far away from the scenery of Ceylon and stared through the canteen window into the dull September afternoon in London.

'You can go to Dorset for the weekend from London, but I cannot go home for another few years.' His voice reflected the pain of separation from home and his people. How much he wanted to complete his studies and run back to his family and…

He could not think further than that, as his heart was aching to see someone. He had no idea in that moment how his past life was going to come to a stop forever. Mary wanted to say that they were both in a new place, starting a new journey. He nodded in agreement.

'I am Paramanathan; please call me Param,' he said in his usual gentle tone.

'I am Mary Vallace, nice to meet you, welcome to London.'

That was their first day.

She spoke of that day, after they had become good friends.

'At first I thought you were an Indian,' she said, as there were a few Indian students around. He smiled and said, 'A few other people have asked me about that, we look the same I suppose.'

A few days later she asked him about the English weather and how he felt about the wind, the cold breeze. Her voice was soft and kind, and while she was talking his mind went back to Jaffna and its music, as Mary's voice reflected the beautiful tone of the *Veena* instrument, which he loved so much.

That memory hit his heart like a sharp arrow from nowhere. When he came to London, he was in a hurry to finish his studies and go back to Ceylon. How did that all change? The name of Ceylon had changed, too, becoming 'Republic of Sri Lanka' to remove the colonial stain.

His father had tried hard to bring up his son as a traditional Hindu boy and arranged his life accordingly. But new social awakening was happening everywhere after the second world war, and many countries were freed from colonialism.

Ceylonese politics, ideologies, were changing, too. The young generation was changing, and their thinking was facing a complete turning from their father's generation.

Falling in love with a girl outside their traditional expectations brought unavoidable complexity into Param's life. The things that were important to him gradually faded away, and unstoppable changes took place beyond his control. Within a few years thoughts of people and places in Sri Lanka had faded.

Now Mary was the most important person in his life. She took care of him and their beautiful ten-year-old daughter Meera, who was forever asking him about his family in Sri Lanka. She had seen plenty of photos of them. His parents, three sisters, a niece and a nephew. That's all he could tell her. But the most important and beautiful image in his heart had to be put away as an unwanted item.

So now, early morning, he was going to leave his loving family in London and face people whom he had not seen for a long time. His family had obeyed his father's order to isolate and punish him for marrying a Christian white girl in London.

Param was in love with a girl in Ceylon before he came to London who was not from a suitable caste according to his father's aspirations. Param's feelings were not a priority. Duty to family, tradition and rituals controlled everyone's lives. Did anyone including his close family in Sri Lanka know what he wanted for himself in his life?

When he was a young man of sixteen and beginning to understand his own identity, he was told by his father, 'You have to be the man of the house sooner or later, as I have only one son, and you to take care of your three sisters and your mother if anything were to happen to me.'

How many young men in the West are told when they are sixteen that they have to take responsibility for the family? His father said that he was worried about the political situation in Ceylon and he was preparing his son to plan for the future for the whole family. Now after many years of separation from his family, their way of life and the girl who'd loved him more than anything in the world, he was suddenly flying back into their world.

Who were the people likely to be waiting for him there in two days? He hadn't seen them for a long time, and his life and family in London made him feel that the family in

Sri Lanka were all strangers to him. He knew their names and faces, but he had no idea of their real feelings towards him, or his towards them.

Param turned back to his wife, Mary. She was fast asleep. He watched her in the dim light through the window for a minute. He loved his family dearly. His loving wife and their clever, beautiful, chatty daughter Meera were his family in England.

The upcoming journey had brought up many memories that hurt him, like a bundle of thorns in his heart.

His steadfast life partner Mary had always kept him from his internal pain, with her true love and their busy life in London. He smiled at Mary's angelic sleeping face. She looked so peaceful and beautiful, her blonde hair spread all over the pillow, her soft face resting on her hand. He wanted to kiss her, but he didn't want to wake her up. He was going to miss her and Meera.

The thoughts of separation from his family created an uneasiness in his mind. He had been so busy for the last few days getting things organised for his trip that there had not been much time to talk about his feelings, and his anxiety about meeting his family in Sri Lanka.

Mary had been working hard to get things ready for his flight, too. She knew he had been asked to come as soon as possible. Param was the only son, and they were expecting him to perform the last rituals for his dying father and be with the mother and family.

Param closed his eyes. He didn't want to feel guilty about not going to Sri Lanka for so many years; but he did. His subconscious mind wanted to stir up things that he didn't want to remember. Sometimes in London he thought about his childhood there, when he saw children playing; there were some nice things for him to remember, but there were also some memories which he'd rather not think back to at all.

Mary had done the spring-cleaning last week. She put away lots of toys belonging to Meera. She doesn't play with them anymore, she said.

Some things you can throw away as soon as you don't need them any longer, but some things you can never throw away because it gives pleasure to have them around.

'I want to look at all the unwanted things and put them away, as I want to get rid of a lot in my past, too,' he wanted to say.

But he watched his wife in silence. Did she know how many painful memories he had put away in order to be a dutiful good husband and a responsible father? And was it important to think about that now?

He could hear the cars pass by in the street. It must be four o'clock in the morning, now. He was tired due to lack of sleep, but he had leave early for the airport.

A few days ago, his elder sister Geetha had phoned him from Colombo, 'If Param wants to do his DUTY to his dying father as an elder son he should come immediately,' she had told him. Would this be his last duty for his family in Jaffna?

Those words from his sister hurt him. Does she think he has no feeling for his father other than doing his duty, not only for him but his sisters, too? Whatever the friction had been between them, he never stopped loving his family. Long before this telephone call he had been told by his baby sister Banu in Jaffna that their father had had a stroke, and Param had immediately started planning the trip to Sri Lanka.

He had already wanted to go home for the summer vacation this year before Meera started secondary school, but Banu's letter and Geetha's phone call had put a rush on his plans.

For a long time he had been wanting to sort out his relationship with his father. But the time was never easy, as there were political problems in Sri Lanka and also his or Mary's work schedules had not allowed them to organise a visit before now.

But as it was Christmas getting a ticket was not that easy. Finally, he'd managed to get a ticket for a Russian flight on Aeroflot, which meant he would have to change in Moscow for another flight to Sri Lanka.

Now, early morning in Islington, North London, he didn't want to think further; if he thought about his mother he would think about his first love Karthiga, too. Father was angry that he married a white woman. Would his parents have been happier if he had gone back to Jaffna and married a low caste girl like Karthiga? No, they would not have allowed him to do that.

He didn't have to look at the empty wall to imagine his beloved Karthiga's 's face. Her face was often there. When he was upset, when he was happy, when he was sad. Whatever he did she always came into his mind. It didn't matter how hard he tried to forget her. It hadn't been easy for a long time, it wouldn't be easy now, either, especially not knowing anything about her current life. His life now was very different from the life he'd led when he was in Sri Lanka. His Sri Lankan family had no influence over him any longer.

He couldn't have slept any more, now. He felt his wife's movements close to him. Her breathing was orderly and systematic, as Mary was a sensible, stable and well organised woman. He pulled his wife towards him tenderly as he wanted to get away from memories of Karthiga.

Mary and Meera were the only family close to him now. He was proud of Mary and adored her administrative skill managing her part time work and married life, and he was often away from home due to his work.

His loving touch woke her up. Mary turned to him, and he kissed her. She opened her eyes sleepily and looked at him. 'Will you miss me?' he asked softly while he was pressing his lips on hers.

She pressed her body close to him. She didn't have to answer that question. Her naked body coiled around him passionately.

'What's the time?' she whispered.

'Sometimes it's better if there is no time at all,' he said softly.

'Make love to me, then darling,' she whispered.

The anticipation of a month's separation made them close and loving. They both felt something extraordinary when they made love. He was going to miss her warm body next to his and her kisses which always enticed him to end up making love to her. He was going to miss her smell, her loving smile, most of all her passion.

'Oh, God, you don't know how much I am going to miss you,' she said. Her nipple was hard and tender, her lips were soft and juicy; he didn't want to go by himself and leave her. Many times they had talked about making love under the moonlight on the golden sandy beach in Sri Lanka.

She said, 'I'll miss you very much, my darling.' Her voice was soft and loving.

'So will I,' he told her while he was completely inside her.

'Will you remember me when you are walking on the sandy golden beach and feeling lonely for love?' She moaned with pleasure when he replied in tune with his movement.

They lay there for a long time without saying much. He wished he could take her and their daughter Meera with him, but he'd made the decision to go home so suddenly that they weren't able to arrange everything. Especially as the political situation in Sri Lanka was not good. In 1977 there were major atrocities against the Tamils by the majority racist Sinhala mobs in Sri Lanka. Many had died, many thousands were internally displaced.

Jaffna town had recently been burned by the Sri Lankan army, Tamil youths were arrested, tortured, some even killed. He didn't want to take his London to his home in Jaffna, yet.

Mary knew he married her without their approval but as time went by, she'd hoped they would accept her. Especially when they had a daughter. She also wanted to meet them, his mother, father and his sisters. Particularly his youngest sister Banu, as Param often said that Meera's beautiful smile often reminds him of Banu. Mary wanted to see the place he was born, the fields he played in, the college where he studied. Even though she had never been to Sri Lanka, she had heard about the island's beauty from others and from him.

'Of course, we will go one day,' he told her many times. But not now.

They stayed in bed silently, and they made love again with much emotion and passion. For him that was his language, his way of expressing his love, and his way of telling his wife how much he wanted her and was going to miss her. Mary often said to him that she preferred his 'particular language', this way of reflecting his love, rather than hearing a speech about love and romance.

He wasn't a person of many words, but a man with honesty and a sense of duty to his family and his profession. They lay there coiled like snakes in each other's arms. His mind wandered immediately to Sri Lanka, thoughts about his father. According to his elder sister Geetha his mother had stopped eating and sleeping, staying at her husband's bedside waiting for him to die peacefully.

Param's breath was so slow while he told her the scenario.

Mary stared at him.

'What's the matter?' he asked, kissing her eyes, which were filling up with tears.

'I don't know.' She just stared at him, like a stranger she had just met.

He preferred not to talk about what he was thinking just then.

They had known each other for many years. They were close and intimate. This was the first time he would be away from her for so long.

'Look after yourself.' She stroked his hair lovingly, like a mother.

He laughed. 'Yes, mum' he replied. They both laughed, now.

'Mary, I'm going to see my mother, remember?' he said.

'I bet you are going to get spoilt by your family in no time, and you will think very little about us while you are there.'

'Do you think so?'

'Daddy.' Meera walked into the room. 'I thought you'd left.' Meera jumped on the bed. Mary put on her dressing gown and went to the kitchen.

'Daddy, will you bring me a big white elephant?' Meera's large brown eyes sparkled.

'Yes, darling, the biggest plastic elephant I can find.' He hugged her and laughed.

Just over ten years old, but she still behaved like a small child at times. Meera looked at him crossly and said, 'I wish you could take me with you, too'

'Some other time, darling'. He kissed her. Meera was a copy of Mary in many ways, but now and then he could see on her face his baby sister Banu's naughty smile. He cuddled his daughter lovingly. Kissed her softly. Leaving her for a long time made him very sad and restless.

'I am going to miss you tomorrow for Christmas, Daddy.'

Meera was looking into his eyes. He felt the sadness in her look. 'Me too, my darling, I am going to miss you and mummy so much.'

His life in London was changed because of Meera. He looked at his daughter and told himself, for the first time in my life I am going to miss these two for a long period. He took a deep breath as if to hold in the loving feeling.

'Will you two get ready?' Mary ordered from the kitchen.

December was coming to an end, but the awful dull weather seemed to have persisted for the past two months. He cleaned the heavy layers of snow from the car. Mary filled the car boot with his suitcase and parcels, while Meera waited in the car. 'I think the traffic is going to be heavy,' Mary said as he got in.

'What else would we expect on Christmas eve, all the last-minute shopping and all. Good Lord, how are we going to make it to the airport in time?' he muttered. He had hoped to travel with no problems.

'We'll manage,' Mary assured him as she brought him back from his thoughts.

None of them knew that it was not only traffic that he would have to struggle through on this trip.

As he started the car his thoughts went back home. 'All these years he had never bothered to come, the only time he comes is when his father is dying.' He knew that his relatives were going to say that. They would be armed with questions for him when he arrived.

He would arrive in Colombo this time tomorrow. Then he would have to take a train to Jaffna in the north.

The traffic on Euston Road was terrible, moving at snail's pace, but the plane wasn't due to depart until twelve noon and it was eight o'clock, so they still had four hours.

'We should have gone by train,' Mary mumbled. 'I hope you won't miss your plane.' she said anxiously, looking at her watch. 'I hope your father is all right, Param.'

She tried to smile at him.

'I hope so, too,' he told her, although he knew that his father was not going to be alright, at all.

Meera was looking out the window. It was still early enough for the streets to be dark. The snow began to fall heavily. The traffic was becoming more congested.

'I hope I put all the presents in the suitcase.' Mary's voice was deep and thoughtful.

Param turned to his wife, and she smiled. She was always so careful about everything.

'Why are you smiling?'

'I love you,' she said.

'Do you?' He raised his eyebrows naughtily.

She hit him softly.

'Come home quickly.'

'I am going to do my duty for my father, but I have no intention of settling in Sri Lanka without you,' he said.

How little did he know that he would be saying the complete opposite when he was there.

'Daddy, shall we go on our summer vacation to see Grandma and Grandpa?' Meera asked from the back of the car.

'Yes, we will go and see all my family and lots of elephants, Meera darling.'

'Tell him I want to see them all, please,' she said sadly.

'Of course, my sweetie, I will tell Grandpa that.' He smiled at his daughter in the mirror.

'Will it be too hot there, now?' Meera's question made him laugh.

'Yes, darling like the summertime in London,' he said.

' So, you'll have a summer vacation there, then,' Meera giggled.

Mary looked at her husband. There was a bit of silence in the car.

'I will be in Colombo and having a spicy breakfast with my sister Geetha's family this time tomorrow,' he told her in an assuring tone.

'Give me a call as soon as you get there, will you?'

'Certainly, but remember Sri Lanka is not England, things are very different. Making a phone call to England may take time, but I will try, my darling.'

As they reached Heathrow airport, the weather suddenly turned brighter, the sky cleared, and the snow seemed to have disappeared.

'I hope the weather will stay clear until you get home,' he said, looking up at the sky.

'Don't worry about us,' Mary replied. 'I hope your plane will take off on time,' she added.

'I hope so, too.'

'See you, Daddy, have a lovely summer there,' Meera shouted behind him as he left. If his mother had been there, she would have said that calling someone behind their back brings them bad luck. He turned back, waved goodbye to his wife and daughter and then disappeared.

# Chapter 2

Not very many brown or black faces on a plane via Moscow to a third world country, he thought. Maybe the Sri Lankans would get on at Moscow. The stewards distributed newspapers, most of them Russian magazines and papers.

The plane was going through snow-covered clouds, and there was some turbulence. There was a couple next to him who spent the whole time kissing—maybe they were newlyweds going to Moscow on honeymoon.

He was tired, the last two days he hadn't slept much. He lay back and closed his eyes; but within minutes he was woken up by the loud sound of a baby crying behind him. He turned to see the mother trying to settle the baby, who was nine or ten months old. The mother was maybe a Sri Lankan woman. She seemed to have a problem settling the baby. He smiled at the mother to show that he sympathised.

'Sorry,' the woman said.

Param remembered his daughter when she was a baby. Meera hadn't liked travelling at all, and Mary had a hard time settling her, too.

He took a magazine in English but couldn't concentrate on it. The baby started to wail again.

'Excuse me,' he turned to see who was calling him. It was a young white woman next to the mother with the baby. She said, 'You can have some of my books to take your mind off it, as they don't have any English papers here.'

She smiled, and he smiled back. She could be an English or American woman on her way to Sri Lanka for her winter holiday. She was holding the baby now whilst the mother was tidying up the baby bag.

'Thanks,' he took the books she gave him and immediately smiled. They were all women's magazines and papers all about women's rights, freedom etc. He turned back and smiled at her again.

'What's the matter?' the white woman asked. Her expression was surprise as he returned her offer so quickly.

'Feminist propaganda?' He smiled at her.

'Not really,' her tone was firm, but her smile was beautiful and friendly. He looked at her, a slender and a beautiful woman with someone else's baby in her arms, who was now falling asleep.

The white woman took her spectacles off and put them in her handbag with one hand whilst holding the baby in the other. She looked so motherly, the way she took care of the other woman's baby. He thought about his caring wife Mary.

'Thank you, anyway' He returned the lot to her.

'Don't you want to read them?'

'I'm not an...' he smiled politely.

'What?'

'I'm not a socialist, or...'

'I see... but you don't have to be a feminist to read about women,' she said nicely, firmly and clearly.

He was not in a mood for any discussion. He wanted to be left alone to examine his own thoughts and how he felt about facing his father and the family in Jaffna. The plane seemed to be going at a snail's pace, and he wanted to reach Sri Lanka as soon as possible.

From London Heathrow to Moscow was nearly four hours, and a change and a flight to Colombo from Moscow may take nine hours, so I will be in Colombo by early morning tomorrow, give a call to Mary from there and take a train to Jaffna in the afternoon.

The air hostesses with their lovely smiles disturbed his thoughts, as he saw the food they were serving. The Russian food was good, but he wasn't hungry. Caviar and wine were unusual for his flight experience up to now; they were tasty, but he couldn't be bothered to finish them.

'I've never tasted caviar before,' the young white woman at the back was telling the mother next to her. She had handed back the baby.

'Neither have I,' the mother was saying.

'Neither have I,' he turned and said to them.

Every time he turned back, his shoulder touched the couple next to him, disturbing their kissing. The baby started to cry again. Now, the stewards had joined in, trying to help the white woman and the baby's mother stop the baby screaming.

'Imagine, this little creature is controlling all of us,' the white woman joked.

'She is not going to like the journey,' the mother gasped.

'Don't worry, she will go to sleep as soon as she runs out of energy to scream,' the white woman comforted her; and sure enough, the baby finally went to sleep. The white woman and the mother started to talk about Sri Lanka.

So, she was going to Sri Lanka, too? Was she going alone or going to meet the man in her life, or was she a trendy feminist wishing to explore the 'uncivilised natives'?

The plane flew above the snow-filled clouds for a while, and some soft Russian music filled the plane. He thought about Mary, her face appeared seductively in his mind, and he felt the fresh memory of making love to her in the morning. His mind immediately went back to his wife and daughter. Knowing he was going to miss them for a while made him sad. He wanted to do whatever his family in Sri Lanka needed and return to his loving family in Islington as quickly as possible.

Flight time to Moscow would be about four hours, he told himself, and he fell asleep for a short time. But there were a lot of noises from the young English men and a couple of girls in the back of the plane. They were laughing and joking, as they were going to exotic places to enjoy the Christmas holiday in the sun.

They landed in Moscow, where it was much colder than London. Minus twenty degrees centigrade, according to the weather announcement in the airport. Thank God he had brought his winter overcoat. He slipped it on and wandered for a while around the airport.

It was different from the way he had imagined the USSR. The airport was filled with foreigners flying via Moscow to parts of Southeast Asia or other places. There were also Russians, drinking vodka and laughing very loudly, but at every corner there was a soldier with a gun: that was very different from London. The Christmas decorations brought his daughter's sad face to mind. 'She is going to wake up and miss me,' he thought.

He was too impatient to look around, anymore. But the flight seemed to be late. He went to the announcement board where he could see the details and hear the announcements. The plane to Colombo would take off in two hours. Why is the plane late? he asked himself. There was an announcement about it but the news was simply 'delayed.'

'Hello.' He turned to see the mother from the plane, standing with the young white woman from the London flight.

'Hello,' he replied.

'Hello, I am Param,' he introduced himself to the young white woman.

He examined her quickly. Her tall slim figure was covered with a few layers of wool, and she was wearing spectacles. She sat down on a bench.

'I'm Elizabeth.'

'Not Elizabeth Taylor,' he interrupted her for a joke.

'Oh no, Elizabeth Baker.' She laughed beautifully. 'Are you a Sri Lankan?'

'Yes, how did you know?'

'I don't have to work hard to guess when you are standing near the announcement board and looking at flights to Colombo.' Her voice was soft and with a pleasant tone, her face friendly and her manner so open and helpful.

'Are you going to Sri Lanka, too?' He asked her. She signalled to him to sit next to her on the bench, and he did.

'Yes, but only stopping for a while to see a friend of mine in Sri Lanka, then I am going to India,' she said.

'I see.' He wanted to know why she was going to India. Maybe she was a spiritualist visiting one of those Hindu *maharishi*s. But he was not in the mood to continue the conversation.

'Are you going on holiday?' he asked her for the sake of asking something.

'No, I am a freelance journalist. I want to write a book on Indian women. I've always wanted to go to India, and only now could I find the time for a visit,' she said happily.

'The Beatles started it,' he said jokingly.

'The Beatles started what?'

'Visiting India to find spirituality, passivity, mystique…'

She laughed loudly. 'I am not looking for spirituality. I am a writer.'

'I haven't met many women writers before.'

'There's nothing special about women writers, we don't wear a special hat to announce ourselves,' she said, giggling.

'What do you write about?'

'Oh, about women and issues related to them.'

'Such as?'

'Well, now that I'm going to India, I may write something about Indian women and their way of life.'

'Why not write about women in England? Haven't British white women got issues to write about?'

'Of course, they have, but I sympathise with eastern women; they have such an unfair deal in life.'

'Oh, really?' He couldn't help but express his displeasure at her understanding of eastern women. 'So, you think women in the east are badly treated but not women in the west?'

'There is oppression everywhere, but at least women in the west have the right to choose.'

'Do they... completely?'

'Well, I don't want to get into an argument about east and west, but for whatever reason I've always been interested in eastern people, particularly in India, I think the caste, culture and traditional way of lives and all are helpful for women and their empowerment.' she said.

He smiled, saying nothing.

The mother with the baby came towards them. 'The toilet is terrible,' the Sri Lankan mother said.

'Oh, Param, this is Mrs. Jeyaratnam,' Elizabeth introduced her.

'Hello, how do you do?' he said, smiling at the mother. Mrs. Jeyaratnam reminded him of his next-door neighbour when he was in Colombo.

'The toilet is terrible, no hot water,' Mrs. Jeyaratnam complained again. 'The Russians should spend some money on toilets rather than on rockets.'

'Governments should think about their people first.' Liz Baker took the baby from her.

There was finally a call for the plane, and all three and the baby boarded. There weren't many people on the flight, and there were two empty seats next to him. Behind him Mrs. Jeyaratnam and her baby sat quietly for a change. Elizabeth came onto the plane with her huge handbag.

Is it full of books? he wondered. He looked at the empty seats next to him. He could tell she wanted to come there so as to be away from the crying baby.

She was studying the empty seats reluctantly.

'They seem vacant,' he pointed to the seats next to him to give the message that he didn't mind if she sat next to him.

'Oh, good.' She sat next to him and placed her heavy bag on the end seat until a stewardess insisted she put it in the overhead luggage compartment. He looked at her, fearing prolonged talks on anything and everything. She got the message clearly from his expression.

'I do not want to sit in the end seat as people who pass by sometimes disturb me.'

'Oh. That's Ok.' He smiled politely.

'Don't worry, I'm not going to give you lectures on feminism and socialism,' she said with a sarcastic smile.

'If you give me a lecture it would be like a lullaby and put me to sleep. I didn't have any sleep last night.' As he was saying this, he remembered his wife's face. Would his family be okay without him?

He turned to look outside. It was so dark. The Moscow city lights flickered though the snow.

'Looking for the Kremlin?' Elizabeth asked.

'Can't see a thing.' He pulled down the shutter.

'Stay in the USSR and you'd see,' she said mockingly to remind him that this is a communist, socialist country.

'No time, and I have no intention, thank you.' His voice was dull. The flight was already two hours late, and he wanted to go to sleep.

He closed his eyes. London and Jaffna superimposed in his mind. Mary and Meera and sick father, mother, three sisters and… He didn't want to think any more, but he couldn't've concentrated on anything else.

How much will have changed? Would Mother look grey, old and ill? Would Father speak to him? Many times his daughter Meera wanted to go to see her grandparents and big elephants in Sri Lanka. Param wanted to take his family to his parents and family, too. But he was unconsciously fearful of his father and reluctant to face him.

His life was turned upside down when he told his father that he was going to marry Mary and be with Mary in London in the future and had no interest in settling in Ceylon.

'How dare you insult me like this?' his father had yelled at him over the phone. 'I brought you up as a decent Hindu young man who put his duty first for the family and our ways of life. But you seem to have no respect for any of what I have being teaching you. You will not see me until I die, because you have brought so many problems to the family with your selfishness.'

For the first time in his life in London Param would have to miss Christmas with his family. Mary wasn't too happy that he was going away without them, but they had no choice. He had never been apart from her up to now.

It was not only his family he'd to break away from because of Mary but also someone else too, in Sri Lanka.

That 'someone else' would be somewhere in Sri Lanka. 'Will I see her?'

The sudden memory of 'someone' in Sri Lanka went through his heart like a sharp knife. Every time he thought about meeting that someone, he felt restless and guilty. Am I thinking and worrying only about my family? he asked himself. Mary could put Meera's unwanted toys away in the attic. What could he do to tidy up the remnants of his past?

What will I do? he asked himself. My past will be right there in front of me.

His mother Amutha was one of the kindest and loveliest people in his life. Who knew, then, why her husband was in such a hurry to send their loving only son Param to London. What would she do when he was in front of her now in Jaffna to carry out the last duty for his father, who had destroyed his love for a beautiful young girl who was not of their caste?

Param knew why his father had insisted he go to London. His mother had been a bit restless as the plan was so sudden. She was happy to see his extraordinarily happy mood whenever he returned from the maths tutor.

His father could ask his mother to keep an eye on him and see whether he was bringing a friend back who was not their caste and status, or if he was reading unwanted books on equality in society or something like that. There was a big movement to abolish the caste and class system in the early 1960s in Jaffna peninsula. He was only nineteen years old, then. She only wanted her son to be happy and not irritate his father. He was her only son.

As far as he knew about her from other people, his mother was from an affluent family, and had a life with servants and privileges when she was in Colombo. When she was eighteen, she came to a family wedding in Jaffna with her parents. Param's father Mr. Sundaram saw her at the wedding. Mr. Sundaram was a man of extreme religious ideologies and traditional attitudes. So, suddenly her life turned upside down when the marriage proposal came from Mr Sundaram's family. Their status and religion all tallied for marriage. That lovely young lady Amutha got married within a year and settled with her husband.

Param's father was an administrator in the Ceylon government from the time of the British colonial administration onwards. He maintained distance from others who were lesser in status and caste. There were a few groups of Tamils in Colombo with a western education and the same attitudes. They were Hindu and Christians, but they came together in their ideology and were better educated than any other Tamils on the island. They would look for a partner from the same circle and, like the Colonial Brits, never wanted to integrate with anyone else.

That all changed when the British left Ceylon in 1948. The majority Sinhala population of Sri Lanka wanted to share power in the political system. Conflicts erupted between Tamil and Sinhala populations, and the first riots in 1958 against the Tamils in Colombo drove them out of Colombo to settle in Jaffna. Param's father returned to work after a few months away from Colombo as he was a prominent figure in the administration. But he left his family in Jaffna as he was fearful of further attacks by racists in Colombo.

As a middle-class Tamil boy, Param's adolescent life in Jaffna was unsettled for a while, as he was a well westernised boy from Colombo, where he had grown up and played with people he'd known since he was a little boy. He was confused, cross and unhappy because the social system in Jaffna was very strict. The caste system was inhumane, as he was not allowed to bring a friend from another caste to his family home. Param's father was back in Colombo, but his mother brought the children up carefully under her husband's instruction.

After a few years in Jaffna, Param's departure to university in Colombo made him happy, not because he was going to university, but because of who was there who would make him happy. And he knew that his mother had noticed how he had changed.

Would his mother cry when she saw him? She was always so emotional. She hadn't eaten for days when he was preparing to come to London. She stayed in the kitchen most of the time with her servant and the cooking equipment, making food and sweets for him to take on the journey. She spent most of her life in there; she thought of nothing but working for her husband and family, as is the duty of a middle-class Sri Lankan Tamil mother. Sometimes the pots and pans were changed or replaced in the kitchen, but not her or her service to her family. She was invaluable to the family structure. She was a good planner, devising and completing tasks carefully as she cooked her spicy meals.

She cried when her husband or the relatives complained about her children. She would go on and on about good and bad or *karma* (sin) and *tharma* (law) in life. She strongly believed that whatever we have to suffer or cherish is all due to karma in our previous life. She had taught the children Hindu philosophy and what they ought to know. She was a religious and class- and caste-conscious woman like any other educated middle-class Tamil woman in Jaffna.

Mother, behind your tears I know you hid so much of your anger over my love for Karthiga because of her caste and class. You thought that it had to do with me being young, not realising that she was my true love. He wanted to tell these things to her when he was with her but he never could. Param was an obedient boy to his parents and their way of life, but when he fell in love, his mind thought nothing regarding the social system but only about the girl he loved.

He knew the real reason his family had wanted to send him to London; his father wanted him to forget about his love for Karthiga.

Oh, Karthiga, he wanted to shout her name.

Would she be married? Would she have any children? How would she react if she sees me? Would she introduce me to her husband, saying 'This is Param, he used to be a colleague of mine at the university of Colombo?' or would she say, 'This is Param, he used to come to my father for tuition, and I would say hello to him?' Or would she say, 'This is Param, he was my first love?' Or would she say, 'This is Param, he broke his promises to me?' Or would she completely ignore him?

Oh, Karthiga, I thought I'd forgotten all about you, but it seems I never could do that, he muttered to himself.

The Russian plane was flying from Moscow to Sri Lanka, and so were his memories.

He remembered the first time he saw Karthiga at her house. He was looking for a maths teacher who could help him pass his university entrance exam, and someone mentioned Mr. Sivam, who was famous in Jaffna for teaching maths. He cycled through the suburb of Jaffna town. When he came to the narrow lane filled with mango trees, he checked the address in his notebook.

It was a beautiful evening. The sun was going down on the west coast, the moon started to come up in the east, the air was cool, the toll of the bell from the temple was musical and soothing.

He looked up, and there was the girl. He was shocked to see her in front of him in the narrow lane. It was the girl who had filled his mind over the past few months. He had first seen her at *Nallur Murugan* temple festival, and she had stolen his heart with her beautiful eyes. So slender a figure, with dark eyes, a round face. Today, wearing a bright blue skirt and blouse, she was chasing a goat. Her hair was long, and it spread all over her shoulders; maybe she had just washed it. She stopped running after the goat when she caught his gaze upon her.

'I am looking for Mr. Sivam Master's house, do you where it is?' he asked her. He forgot that Jaffna young girls are not allowed to talk to strangers. But he was amazed to see her in front of him, after a few months of also seeing her at the temple.

She smiled. 'This is the house,' she said. Her voice was so soft and clear like the tone of the classical instrument of *Veena*. She walked through the gate. The goat had already disappeared behind their house.

There were so many days that followed with only a smile between them. She would appear and disappear now and then, and his heart beat fast whenever he saw her. He knew she was not allowed to talk to a young man alone. She was a Hindu girl, and as a young virgin she had a strong tradition to follow.

They both eagerly awaited every single evening just to look at each other. Now and then, he passed a remark on her long hair or her sparkling dark eyes which haunted him day and night, then millions of things happened.

What would she say, now? He had not wanted to think about those things after he met Mary, but now he couldn't stop the memories coming back, like ghosts haunting him.

Most people on the plane were sleeping, including baby Jeyaratnam. Miss Liz Baker's book was open on her lap and she was asleep, too, nearly falling on his shoulder now and then when the flight shook. Miss Baker was very young, maybe twenty-six or a bit more. Most of the young women he knew were reserved and very rarely talked to strangers first. Liz Baker seemed different. Her kindness towards the mother and baby and her open and sweet mannerisms made it easier to talk to her. He watched her silently and thought about Mary.

Would they be okay? he asked himself again. The car needed repairing. Mary needed the car to go to work and take Meera to school. His thoughts of the family stopped when the plane shook a bit and Miss Baker's head nearly hit his shoulder.

But it didn't seem to bother her, and she slept comfortably, unaware that she was almost sleeping on someone else's husband's shoulder. She seemed settled into a deep sleep, but her warm breathing into his neck made him uncomfortable. He suddenly remembered kissing Mary and making love the night before.

Elizabeth's blonde hair reminded him of Mary's long hair. He liked women with long hair, he loved fiddling with Mary's hair. His thoughts of Mary stopped as the plane gave a sudden shake and began preparing to land. Elizabeth got up and looked at him in confusion.

'What happened?' she asked him sleepily.

'I don't know. I am not a pilot. I am one of you, you know,' he joked, but he was irritable, realising something had gone wrong.

The captain made some announcement in Russian. What was going on? The passengers looked at each other.

'Who can understand Russian?' Miss Baker said angrily.

It was funny watching the English faces, thinking that English is 'the master's voice—everywhere in the world', but out of England it was a very different story.

The English translation came later, saying that because of unavoidable circumstances the plane was having to land. Until the situation was settled, passengers were asked to stay at the airport.

'How long is it going to take? I should have gone by BOAC or Singapore, or taken Air India,' Miss Baker mumbled.

'Why didn't you?' Param asked.

'Well, I took this flight because the fare was cheap.' She looked fed up.

'You are not in a hurry, are you?' he asked her.

'Not really, that is not the point. I just hate to waste time doing nothing.'

'Oh yes, who wants to waste time, especially in strange airports?'

'Are you in a hurry?' she asked him.

He nodded his head to indicate 'yes'. His father was dying. Of course, he was he in a hurry to see his dying father.

After a few hours of confusion and angry remarks by the passengers, there was an announcement in English. Because of some problem with flying over Tehran due to diplomatic matters with Iran, the flight had to await permission to fly over another country. So, the passengers would have to wait.

'No wonder,' Miss Baker remarked.

'What?' Param was not interested in the USSR or any other politics.

'You see, there was news in the paper a few days ago, that some Russian diplomats were being expelled from

Tehran, accused of spying or something. It may be because of that that we have to suffer now.' Liz Baker continued.

Mrs. Jeya's baby was sleeping for a change. There were a few more Tamils; they came over and talked to Param. They had come from African countries, or Norway or Sweden. There was a Tamil woman who was teaching in Zambia and was having difficulty with her enormous hand luggage.

Then came an announcement saying the plane would have to make an unscheduled stopover in Tbilisi, in Georgia.

'Really, this is too much.' Param was fed up with waiting. Not being with his father at that moment irritated him. He hadn't had any sleep at all the night before, and now it was nearly four am in the morning Russian time. People were tired and sleepy, and there wasn't much information coming from the authorities at all.

He sat very quietly and thought about Mary. She might be awaiting his call from Colombo now, but what could he do?

The sun rose reluctantly from behind one of the hills through the slightly foggy Christmas morning, as the plane landed at Tbilisi instead of Colombo airport. Tbilisi was the capital city of Georgia in southern Russia, they were told. It was a beautiful place. The airport was surrounded by mountains and hills. But he couldn't care less where he was. The only thing he wanted to do was to get out of there.

There was not much food or drink on the plane. Tbilisi was a small domestic airport, unable to cater for international travellers, so re-stocking the plane was not feasible. The stewards passed out packets of peanuts, but the passengers were not pleased.

'Oh what a fucking Russian breakfast for Christmas morning'? One of the English young men was shouting from the back of flight, and the young English crowd was furious that their exotic South Asian holiday schedule was being disrupted by some mishap of the Russians.

His thoughts flew immediately to Islington, would Mary be preparing to cook for the Christmas dinner, now? He forgot for a minute that he was in flight to Sri Lanka. 'They are going to be alone today.' He was not there to see Meera's sparkling eyes when she opened her presents. He was going to miss Mary's delicious Christmas lunch and her proud smile when he passed his remarks about her cooking.

'I'm starving,' Miss Baker mumbled. Her face looked very tired and pale.

'Fasting is good for body and soul,' he said, trying to be cheerful.

'I don't think I will live in a communist country,' she declared.

'I don't think we will get an invitation.' This sarcasm didn't cheer her up, and she turned her face the other way. He couldn't work out whether she was angry or shy.

There was an announcement that the plane would take off soon and the passengers should buckle their seatbelts. A sigh of relief rippled through the passengers, but still the plane didn't take off.

It was nearly midday now; he imagined the Christmas day celebration in London. Most of the passengers in the plane were angry from lack of sleep and lack of food. Some English youngsters got into a big argument, using bad language to express their anger with the Russian stewards.

'Open the bloody door, I am going to Moscow by train,' one English young man shouted. He wanted to go to the British High Commission to complain about the treatment he had received.

'I don't think there is anything wrong with the aircraft. Maybe they are using the plane to bomb some place or take troops to Afghanistan or something,' Miss Baker remarked irritably to Param. She doesn't like Russians, he thought, but he was in no mood to argue.

At about seven in the evening, there was another announcement saying that they did not know when the plane would be able to take off. Passengers would have to disembark and be taken to a tourist hotel somewhere in the city.

'Oh no, it can't be true,' Elizabeth's voice was sad and angry.

Param should have been on the train to Jaffna by now. He understood Liz's anger. But she was not on her way to participate in some important diplomatic conference, was she? She was just going to spend time in India looking for women to talk to and write a book, why was she in a hurry? But he thought it best not to let her know his thoughts.

As they disembarked at the airport in Tbilisi city, a bewildered official issued them all emergency tourist visas, and they dragged their baggage through a Customs barrier which had been erected just for them.

When they reached the hotel, the staff looked puzzled and confused to see a big crowd of foreigners in the early part of Christmas night. Everything was chaos. Most of the hotel staff did not speak English at all, which made it difficult to communicate. The receptionist with her broken English asked for details from the passengers and allocated the rooms.

He wanted to phone Mary and let her know what was happening, but there were no public phones in the lobby. He didn't know whether to ask for a public phone, or to wait in case the flight was called to take off. Then they were told they would not be able to phone home, but no one explained why. As it had been a through flight, no one had any Russian currency, so sneaking off to find a payphone was out of the question, as there were security guards everywhere to control the emergency situation. Passengers were queueing up to register and to find about their accommodation.

Param went to the restaurant and asked for a cup of tea. It took about half an hour to get through to the waiter to make him understand.

But they were given dinner after an hour or so. Lots of wine and not a lot of food but there was plenty of caviar. Young English people were enjoying the wines. Param could not give much thought to food or wine at the moment. He wanted to rest and prepare to travel to Colombo as soon as possible from Tbilisi.

The lift was full of people, happy-looking Russians. Like the Moscow airport, most seemed jolly and noisy as they were celebrating Christmas. He noticed that most of the middle-aged Georgian women were slightly larger than English women. He thought about Miss Baker and her slender figure. Where would she be? Maybe somewhere on the fortieth floor or somewhere with Mrs. Jeyaratnam and her crying baby, who knows?

He opened the door to his room; it wasn't locked. He was shocked to see Miss Baker there, already settled into a beautifully made double bed with attached bathroom facilities. It was a honeymoon suite. He said, 'Oh no.' She got up, surprised. He had his card. Room number twenty-seven.

She looked at her card. 'Yes, it is room number twenty-seven,' she said. 'They can't have put both of us in the same room,' she nearly cried.

He laughed nervously at her anger, which made her face more red and cross.

'I'm too tired to find this funny,' she barked.

'Well…' He hesitated. He wanted to say, why don't you sleep in the bed, I'll sleep on the settee? But he didn't say anything.

'Well, what?' she questioned. She looked beautiful although she was confused, vulnerable and puzzled. She noticed his gaze, too, and turned her face away.

'Well, I'll go down and see whether they could give me another room.' She got up.

'No, don't you go. I will go,' he volunteered, turning toward the door.

'What are you going to do if they put you in with another woman?' she questioned. Was she joking or what?

Param wanted to ask her, what you think I should do? Make love passionately to a strange woman in a Russian hotel like James Bond?

They both went down to the front desk, where they saw Mrs. Jeyaratnam with a Russian man. She had needed some help with the baby—so she'd found someone who could speak English. The man listened to his argument and looked at his card, and asked, 'Why can't you sleep together? This card says that you are a couple.'

The three travellers from London laughed. The receptionist had asked them questions, but they hadn't understood her, so she had assumed that Mr. Sundaram and Ms. Baker were together.

'The 'Ms' in front of my name must have given it away,' she said.

'I have a double room,' Mrs. Jeya said to Liz Baker. 'You can stay with me'.

Back in the room, Ms. Baker jokingly said, 'I hope you get some sleep, as long as they don't send another female to keep you company,' as she put her things in her bag. He was not in mood to laugh for her joke. She remembered him saying that he had not have much sleep the night before.

'I hope you get some sleep with that crying baby,' he smiled back at her.

He settled to sleep but couldn't.

Two nights ago he was with his wife; last night in the plane Miss Baker used his shoulder to sleep; tonight he was alone. Tomorrow he would be with his sister's family in Colombo and taking the train to Jaffna. There was too much to think about. He got up and put the light on and tried to find something to read, with no luck as there was nothing in English in the room. He went to the window and settled his mind on the street which was sparkling with Christmas lights. There were hundreds of cars and still lots of people about.

The image he had about the USSR was very different from what he was experiencing in Tbilisi. The people had happy faces and were very friendly, although there was a uniformed person with a gun at every corner.

He wanted to go for a walk, so he changed his clothes and went down.

# Chapter 3

Ms. Baker was sitting in a chair in the corner of the hotel reception. The young crowd of English boys with a couple of girls were heading to the lift, swearing and cursing the Russians for not having a bar open. There were a few men in the corner of the big lounge and a few passengers sitting and talking very loudly. Liz seemed to have a book on her lap, but she was staring around at nothing in particular. For some reason Param felt sorry for her being alone there in a strange place in the early morning and not knowing the next move of her journey. She did not join the young English young people. All the time she seemed to stay with either Mrs. Jeyaratnam or with Param. Is she scared of travelling alone? he asked himself before going towards her.

'Are you all right?' he asked her in a worried voice.

She looked up. The tone of his words made her smile. A polite and acknowledging concern for her.

'I couldn't sleep, and I do not want to disturb the baby by fiddling with my books, as the baby is asleep at the moment for a change. Mrs. Jeyaratnam said her family lives in London, she's going to her sister's wedding and was busy for the few days buying things and getting ready to travel to Colombo, so she is tired, too. I came down for a cup of tea but the restaurant is shut. I thought I'd try reading something.'

'I couldn't sleep, either,' he said.

There were two men in the corner looking at Param and Liz in an unfriendly manner. The crowd of men's voices were getting louder. Param did not want any interaction with that kind of crowd. There were a couple of guards with guns at the entrance, keeping eyes on everyone inside.

'I thought I'd go out for a walk. Will you join me?' he asked her.

Outside he could see the colourful Christmas decorations and the merriment of celebration. He missed his family in London. He wanted to walk around the Tbilisi streets on Christmas night to keep his mind from worrying.

She hesitated for a minute and looked around to understand the situation clearly and said, 'I don't think we're allowed.'

'Why not?'

'I asked them, already. They say we are not allowed to, because our visas stipulate that we're not allowed to go out unaccompanied, and we may be taken to the airport any time.'

'Holy shit,' Param mumbled.

'I am uneasy, here. I think something big is going on somewhere in this country. That's why they are watching us. Particularly as we're from London,' she said in a tone of fear.

He sat down near her. He did not want to leave her alone there. He felt something uncomfortable about the two men in the far corner. Were they watching the passengers from Britain? Oh well, what else would you expect from a communist country, he told himself, but did not share his thoughts with Liz Baker.

'Do you want any books?' she asked him.

'Unless it's something very interesting I don't think I could concentrate on reading anything,' he replied hiding his anxiety about the situation.

'Mm, I don't carry books like…'

'I didn't think you would carry novels by…' He did not complete the sentence, which he thought would cheer her up in a strange place at midnight. She interrupted him and, feeling offended, said, 'I am a feminist.'

'So?'

'I am against...'

Now he interrupted her and said, 'Sorry, I didn't mean it that way, I just wanted to make the situation bearable.' His tone reflected his anxiety over the delay.

'We'd better go back up.' She was looking at the guard, who was watching them and also the men in the corner.

They got into the lift. What a strange situation I am in, he thought, and felt uneasy. Mary would have phoned the travel agency in London and understood his situation, he assured himself, to try and feel positive.

He thought about Mrs. Jeyaratnam with a small baby, would her family in Sri Lanka know what is going on about their flight?

Did Miss Baker have any family, or a boyfriend to worry about? He wanted to ask her, but he couldn't. He was not an extrovert with the ability to talk to women easily, and he didn't want her to think something unpleasant about him if he asked her about a personal matter. After all, they'd met only two days ago, in a strange situation. But he felt as though he'd known her for a long time, and he liked beautiful, young, kind, friendly Miss Liz Baker. A loving remedy for his anxiety of mind.

She was different from the English women he knew. He worked with many and was married to one. Some of the white women working with him tended to be a bit less friendly because of his colour; the women who were friendly with him were more like Liz, broad-minded and sincere.

He said goodnight and went to his room. Shortly after, there was a knock on the door. Miss Baker brought him some magazines.

'Mrs. Jeya's women's magazines, not about feminism, socialism or any revolution, so you can learn to cook a good meal while we are in Russia.' She laughed and left them on his table. He thought she was restless in the hotel and wanted to talk to him to pass the time. Was she scared being here in a Russian hotel alone? He thought she was making a joke to create a lighter atmosphere, when she talked about the cookery book.

He looked at the magazines and said, 'Oh no, I don't read them, I'm just worried about my father,' he said sadly.

'Is your father ill?'

'Yes, that's why I am so restless wasting my time here. I couldn't get any other ticket, and now I'm suffering because I've travelled by Aeroflot. I am sorry, Miss Baker, if I have offended you with my silly jokes or...'

She interrupted him and said, 'I am so nervous being here, too. I am sorry, I hope your father is okay. Please call me Liz,' she said kindly. Then she said, 'Mrs. Jeya's little baby seems not well. I hope we can get out of this place as soon as possible, I am really scared.' Her voice crackled with emotion because of the chaos of the last two days.

Suddenly he wanted to touch her and comfort her. He felt something else was scaring her in here. The group of men in the lounge were not friendly-looking, nor were the two men in the corner. Who were they? Stupid men prying on a lonely young woman, or some sort of special agents who think she is a spy or something, travelling through Moscow?

She was still standing there. He wanted to tell her to sit down, but he did not do that in case she thought he was trying to take advantage of her confused situation. He smiled at her, and her expression seemed to relax a little.

She said, 'We have a plane full of strangers, but I think only a few of us are in a hurry to reach our destiny, look at the young crowd who are going to India and Thailand or somewhere, they are missing some days, in Russia, but not the whole purpose.' He did not understand why she was talking about destiny. Was she worried about the men in lounge?

'I hope the flight will leave soon and you will get to Jaffna to see your father.' She smiled like a loving and a sincere friend.

Her kindness and gentle manner soothed him. He wouldn't have minded spending all night just talking to her and comforting her, if she wouldn't mind. But Param was a man who would never ask a young woman to sit in his room in a strange country to talk all night.

He thought back to the time he had met Mary in strange circumstances. Many years ago Param and Mary's relationship made their lives take a completely different turn. Up till then they were just friends, saw each other, and sometimes went out for meals with other students. He spent his first Christmas in London alone at the student hostel. When she came back for the new term, she felt sorry for him to be alone during the Christmas holiday.

She invited him to her house in Dorset during the Easter break with other friends for her twenty-first birthday party. He was surprised to see her parents' faces when they arrived at the door.

Her family may never have had a 'coloured' visitor in their house before. But after the initial shock they treated him kindly. He had his first experience of being with an English family in England. Mary's mother was like her daughter, she was kind and felt sorry for him being alone in London with no family and only a few Sri Lankan friends. He told them he had an uncle who was a doctor in Wales, but that he had gone back to Sri Lanka for the Easter holidays.

During 1968 there were many incidents of attacks on Blacks and Asians in London. The year he came to London

Enoch Powell gave his 'Rivers of Blood' speech in Birmingham. The situation against coloured, and Irish, people was not healthy at that time. When an Asian or Black person looked for a house, they saw openly displayed boards which said 'Flat to Let: Two rooms, Shared bathroom, Kitchenette, £8.00 Weekly. 'No Coloured. No Irish. No Children.'

Param stayed in the student accommodation for a while to avoid any unpleasantness with white racists. The atmosphere around foreigners in London made him want to return to Ceylon as quickly as he could.

Anyway, at that time Param had no intention whatsoever to settle in London. He wanted to run back to his love in Ceylon as fast as possible. He had just over year to complete his study.

One day in late December 1968, just after the Christmas holiday, it was a very cold and windy night. Mary, Param and some other university friends went for a meal. After their friends left to go to the pub. Mary and Param were walking along a London street towards Param's student hostel about midnight. They were chased by a few white thugs who hated to see a white girl in public with a 'coloured' boy. Param did not expect this in the middle of London. They ran fast to the underground station to escape. He was unlucky and had an accident while going down the steps so fast. He fell and hit his head on the concrete steps. He was bleeding heavily, and lost consciousness. Immediately, Mary was screaming for help. Param had a head injury. How long he was unconscious in hospital? Who was holding his hand and stroking it gently, saying, 'You will be OK'? It was like a dream, partially knowing and partly a clouded memory.

He had only a few relatives in England at that time. His university informed his next of kin, the doctor in Wales.

That was his uncle, his mother's brother who'd just returned from Ceylon and came to see him in hospital.

The hospital doctors told the uncle that Param was brought in to hospital just in time to save his life, but he was getting better and would be out soon. Param's uncle thanked Mary for taking care for him. Param did not know that; he was not knowing much around him.

Mary was at his bedside most of the time, he was told by his friends later on. If she had not walked with him that night, Param wouldn't have had anyone to help him as he ran for his life on that dark, snowy night in London. She walked with him and saved his life. He thanked her many times for that. When he was well enough to be discharged Mary asked him to join them in the house she shared with a few students from her class.

'Good night.' Liz brought him back from his thoughts to the present.

'Sorry, I was miles away, thinking,' he apologised. He was suddenly confused as he could see Liz as Mary in front of him, gentle and kind.

'I can tell by the way you looked at me,' she went to the door. Her smile was pleasant and invitingly beautiful.

He felt that he must protect her while they were stranded on Russian soil with strangers. Liz was an exceptionally kind woman who was taking care of Mrs. Jeya and her baby as if she had known them all her life, rather than joining the young English people and enjoying with caviar and wine.

Param thought Liz had a special way of talking to people, with no barriers at all. She was a journalist and may have had plenty of experience of intriguing circumstances. Surely no man could resist wanting to spend time with her, and probably no woman could resist being friendly with her because of her kind manner. He thought about Liz a lot that night.

Some slept, some dreamed; the night went by in the wonderful Tbilisi hotel, surrounded by beautiful mountains and ancient buildings. He stood at the window and stared at the night world of Tbilisi. The city looked amazing. He felt he was in a dream world with the fantastic colours of Christmas decorations and the magnificent buildings. And the lighting from the buildings of all kinds such as hotels, churches and fortresses around the Tbilisi high hills made the place seem unreal, unique and special, far from the reality of London or Sri Lanka.

The next day the weather was lovely, and the airline's authorities took them on a sight-seeing tour. The two men who were in the hotel the night before were there in the bus, too. Mrs. Jeyaratnam did not come on the tour as her baby was not well.

Param felt an uneasiness about the way the two men were looking at the English passengers, particularly Liz. 'Do they think that she is pretending to be a journalist? Do they think she is here to spy on them? What a stupid idea that would be.' He was worried about Liz, but she seemed to be happy about the trip.

Liz sat next to Param and enjoyed the tour. Tbilisi had been invaded by many powers in the past, and that was reflected in the architecture of the buildings. There were Persian traits and middle Eastern styles, and all blended together in the making of beautiful Tbilisi. When they went to Narikala fortress the guide explained that that fortress was the 'soul and heart of the city'. They weren't allowed to get out of the bus much. Some passengers complained to the guard and asked them whether they were treating the passengers as political prisoners. Is this what one expects here?

'After all, Georgia is the place where Joseph Stalin was born, so the guards may be following their late master's order to keep watch on everyone,' Liz mumbled quietly.

People in the bus were enjoying the magic of Tbilisi.

Trinity Cathedral towered into the blue sky to tell the visitors about the deep Christian faith of Georgia. The magnificent bridge took their breath away with its elegant style and surroundings.

Liz spent most of the tour photographing the most beautiful scenery from every angle. But there were places where the guard stopped her taking photos. She hadn't expected that. But she was determined to enjoy the journey. She looked amazingly gorgeous in that extraordinary scenery.

'This is the oldest bridge in the world,' the Georgian tour guide was telling them proudly over the microphone. 'Miss Baker,' Param called, beckoning her toward the bridge. 'Please call me Liz,' she said kindly.

He could tell that the people around them were thinking they were a couple on holiday or something, when Liz spoke to him in a highly excited tone.

But suddenly, he thought about Mary and Meera being there with him.

He would have loved to take Meera there and see her big brown eyes fill with joy and happiness at this place.

Liz reminded him of his family. She had a child-like smile, and she laughed a lot.

Mary wouldn't laugh loudly in front of people. Liz seemed to enjoy nature, maybe that is the way with writers, he thought.

'I wish I could spend more time here,' she said.

'You said you wanted to take a train to Moscow to complain to the British High Commission.'

'Yes, yes, I did, when we were sitting in the airport, but this is beautiful.' Her voice was so happy, her eyes sparkling. Seeing her beauty in this extraordinary atmosphere made him feel he wanted to spend more time with her and talk to her about anything or nothing, but just be with her.

But he also felt uncomfortable about his thoughts of Liz. He had no intention to make Liz think less of him. He realised that his mind was restless and seeking comfort from her. That may lead to misunderstanding, he thought.

'I just wanted to get to Colombo,' he said in a sad tone, and he thought his father might have died already, and the family had carried out the funeral rituals without him.

'Oh, I am sorry to be so selfish,' she apologised.

The food wasn't that bad in the hotel, but staying in a strange city for five days with no explanation was too much. The passengers started to argue and fight with the authorities.

'Do you think the Russians are invading somewhere in the south?' she asked him with fear in her voice.

Invading somewhere? His stomach turned upside down with fear and worry. They were told that there was a problem in flying over Tehran due to some diplomatic showdown. Oh no, please don't keep us any longer here, I will go mad. He wanted to yell at the officers.

After lots of shouting and arguing by the British passengers, the situation was getting serious. A few hours after the verbal battle, a plane was arranged, and they took off for Colombo.

From London to Moscow, then the stop at Tbilisi, the six days with Liz and going to see the beautiful places in the city made him closer to her, as if they had been friends for many years. They talked about various topics, feminism, politics and some things that didn't have any particular topic, they just talked, joked, and laughed. She released the tension caused by his worries. He thanked her for being friendly towards him and easing the worries and the tension he felt.

She thanked him for taking care of her. Taking care of you? He questioned her with surprise as he had never thought that that was what he was doing since he saw the unfriendly looking two men staring at her a few nights ago in the hotel lounge and following them around.

'So, you think I didn't notice at all?' she giggled like a teenager.

He did not answer her but wanted to say, 'I am a brother of three girls, a father and a husband, too, I know how to keep on eye on ladies in front of unfriendly and vulgar minded men'.

'You are a kind man, my dear Param. I am glad that I met you,' she said with a motherly tone and with one of her amazing smiles. 'We have lost six days in Russia, but...' She did not continue her sentence but stared at him deeply for a few seconds and said, 'I am very happy that I have met you. What we lose, sometimes we gain something else to please us.'

Those words shocked him for a second. He had lost his first love in Ceylon a very long time ago, and he had gained a loving family in London. Liz was talking about a few days in Russia.

He was a strictly married man who'd never had the time nor the opportunity to be with other women. Liz made him feel young and happy. She was an intelligent woman with the kind of assertive personality that made men get excited, and he found it hard to resist. He had found someone so special, close, and sincere. His mind wandered about his feelings towards her.

Life can go on the same for a long time, and suddenly everything can change within a short period, when you meet someone or come across an unexpected experience, he told himself when he was talking to Liz. He felt something for her, some connection with her, which he couldn't understand.

The flight took over to Sri Lanka. Ceylon's name had changed in 1972. The air steward announced that they would be landing at Bandaranayake Airport soon. He was landing in Sri Lanka after six days of chaos, fear and unexpected friendship with Liz. He looked through the window of his beloved country which he had missed for many years. Through the window it seemed such a little island from the sky, a pearl in the Indian Ocean, that's true.

'It is so beautiful. You are so lucky to have been born in this country,' Liz, next to him, exclaimed.

'Lucky to be born in Sri Lanka as a Tamil?' He questioned his position. After 1977, following riots against the Tamil minority in Sri Lanka, thousands of Tamils sought political asylum elsewhere in the world. How much did she know about the situation for Tamils?

'I don't know how people can live away from this beautiful country.'

'Beauty doesn't give peace or freedom to Tamils in Sri Lanka,' he said quietly. He didn't like politics, and he never wanted to talk about political issues. He was a humble man with simple aims in life. Study, then marriage; now he had a family. That's all he knew.

'That's all?' said a voice in his mind. He looked out of the window.

'I'd like to see you in Colombo,' Param told her as they landed.

Already the temperature was about eighty degrees Fahrenheit, like a very hot summer in London.

Would Karthiga be in Colombo? She was living there when he left her many years ago. She had been teaching near Colombo. Would she still be living in the same place? He had never before wanted to look for the answer, but now those questions repeated in his mind over and over again.

'I'd like to meet up, but I will be staying in Kandy for a while, before returning to Colombo,' Liz said.

'Well, maybe we will meet again sometime in London,' he said.

He shook her hand. It was soft and small.

'Mary, my wife, would like your philosophy of feminism.'

'Oh, you didn't tell me you were married.'

He looked at her for a while and said, 'I don't advertise it.' He smiled, and wanted to ask her whether he was behaving as a wild unmarried man while he was with her alone in so many beautiful places in Tbilisi and in the room? But he did not as he did not want to spoil the loving friendship made in the uncertain environment.

'It was nice in Russia. It would have been so boring if I had been alone,' she said, without looking at him. A cold chill went through his mind, as he was thinking the same thing at exactly the same time.

'Yes, it was, but I was a bit restless, really.' Which was true.

'I noticed; now, I know the reason,' she said softly.

He smiled at her; she turned her face away.

No one was waiting for him at the airport in Colombo. They might have waited a few days ago, but how were they to know that he would get stuck in the USSR?

Liz did not have anyone waiting for her. She said she had told her friend that she was going to stay in Colombo for a while. Then she would go to Kandy.

They both exited the airport.

'It feels so strange to be here,' he said. He was remembering Sri Lanka and its atmosphere, beauty, smell and tranquility from such a long time ago. He looked up at the clean sky, blue and bright, in complete contrast to London's dull grey.

The heat was making her fan herself with a paper. 'Too hot,' she said.

'My daughter said I should have a summer vacation here'.

'Yes, we should; it's a beautiful place for a summer vacation,' Liz said.

'Mmm,' he mumbled, thinking he should go and see his father as soon as possible. He asked her if she wanted to come with him in the taxi.

Liz said goodbye to the Jeyaratnams, saying she would meet them when she returned from Kandy in a few days' time. Mrs. Jeyaratnam asked Param to visit her family in Colombo when he had time, and she gave him her telephone number and house details.

'If I can't visit you here, please come and visit my family in Islington, since you live in London, too,' he said politely.'

'I'd love to visit you, Mr. Param, you were kind to us during our difficult journey,' Mrs. Jeya told him with a grateful voice.

'We cared for each other,' he replied to her.

Liz sat next to Param in the taxi.

He told her which hotel to go to in Colombo and asked the driver to take them there. The taxi went down Negambo Road towards Colombo. There were many changes, new buildings, roads and tourist hotels—but Sri Lanka still looked calm and beautiful.

'No wonder people call it Paradise Island.' Liz was completely absorbed by Sri Lanka's breathtaking natural beauty.

'You will forget the whole world when you see the really beautiful scenery in the central part of Sri Lanka,' he said. She stayed silent.

'People should go with their...' He couldn't finish the sentence. He vividly remembered Karthiga's face when they went together to see the scenery in the highlands.

'Go with their lovers, do you mean?' she asked quietly, not looking at him.

They had only known each other for a few days, but they seemed to understand each
other's thoughts. 'I suppose so,' he said.

'Well, I will bring my Mr. Right if I ever find one,' she said jokingly, but he noticed the sadness in her voice. So, she was not attached to anyone.

He wanted to go with her to wherever she was staying and take her out to see the most beautiful sights of Sri Lanka. But he knew he had to phone Mary and rush to see his dying father. He got out on Galle Road in the Wellawatta area, and they exchanged their London telephone numbers and addresses. He gave her his Colombo address.

'I hope we will meet again,' he said as he got out of the car, and they held each other's hands for a while. It had been like a dream for him to be with her in Russia; now the dream was over, and the reality was the uncertain future ahead of him.

'Oh, if we don't meet here, we will meet up in London,' she gave him one of her charming smiles. He stood on the side of Galle Road and watched the taxi depart.

'Will I ever see her again?'

# Chapter 4

His elder sister Geetha's house at Nelson Place in Colombo looked partly burned down and damaged. He hesitated for a minute, wondering whether he was looking at the right house as there was no one around. Usually at this hour the house would be open, the children playing outside; that was the memory he had.

He was born in this house and grew up here until the 1958 riots against the Tamils in Colombo, then the Tamils had run to Jaffna for safety.

The lanes used to house many Tamil families, their children playing in front of their houses while their mothers chatted; he looked around again as he walked towards the house. He rang the bell reluctantly. The door opened.

'Hey, come and see who is here,' his brother-in-law called back excitedly.

Immediately, his elder sister Geetha and her two children appeared with surprised faces.

'Oh, what a worry you gave me. Aeroflot gave us absolutely no information.' His sister came and held onto his arm warmly, a sisterly expression on her face and tears in her eyes. He was her only brother. Her touch was soft and gentle as she held on to him as she used to do when they were small children.

'How is Father?' he asked her.

'He is still hanging on, he is a stubborn man, but we have to leave soon,' his sister said.

'I am so sorry for the delay, for some reason they could not fly out of Tbilisi for days,' he said to his sister in a sad tone.

'We have been waiting for you for five days. Your wife has phoned a few times. We phoned the Aeroflot office, and they told us the plane was delayed, but they didn't know when the replacement flight would arrive.'

He sat on the sofa and tried his London number immediately, but he couldn't get a line straight away. He wanted to hear his wife's and daughter's voices. He knew Mary would be worried now; she would be delighted to hear from him.

'This is not London. You can't just get an international line as soon as you dial,' his sister scolded. 'It will take them a few hours to give you a connection.'

His sister asked the children to get the table ready for a meal, and she quickly got things out to prepare him something good to eat; she was a good cook. He saw the warm welcome from his sister's family and felt wanted, loved so much by them. He had missed this feeling of my family for a long time. What he had missed for nearly twelve years.

He'd stayed with his sister Geetha and her husband when he was at Colombo university, and she had taken care of him as if he were her own child, although there was only three years' age difference between them.

'Do you remember this little creature?' his brother-in-law pointed out the young woman next to him at the lunch table. She looked about fourteen and rather shy of meeting his gaze.

'Of course, I remember naughty little Sandra.' Param smiled at the young lady, his niece Sandra who was hiding behind his sister. 'Sandra had the loudest cry in the neighbourhood when I was here last time.'

Param's remarks made the young girl even more shy. He talked about her babyhood affectionately, they all laughed for a while.

'What about this?' His brother-in-law pulled the young boy in front of Param.

'Well, he was the lump my sister was carrying, am I right? It wasn't just a lump but a very big one that was making my sister throw up a lot.' Param's remarks made everybody laugh again.

'You were so kind to look after me, then,' his sister's voice indirectly asked him how he had managed to stay away from them for all these years. In his ears he could hear, what Liz was telling him a little while ago, how 'kind' he was.

'Well, if you get ready, we can catch the afternoon train to Jaffna.' Param's sister had nearly finished cooking, and the smell made his mouth water.

'How's the family?' his brother-in-law asked him the customary question.

'They are both well. Meera wanted to come with me, but as I had to come so quickly, I didn't want to drag her along.'

His sister's food was good, spicy and tasty.

'I thought you wouldn't be eating any spicy food,' his sister remarked as she watched him eat happily.

'Why not? England has lots of Indian shops where you can buy almost anything. It wasn't easy in the days when I first went to London, but now London is a cosmopolitan city.'

His niece and nephew took some time to get over their shyness and talk to him, but once they started, nothing could stop them, asking question after question about London, 'the great city of the world'. They didn't ask much about his wife or daughter.

Param looked around his sister's house. What he had noticed from the outside earlier he could see more clearly now, the damage. She was aware of his question from his look before he had even thought to ask.

'That's the evidence of the general election in 1977.' His sister's eyes were full of tears. 'Thank God, you were away. Tamils are going through hell because of this racist government,' she continued to explain, while serving the food.

He had seen news about Sri Lanka on British television, but now he was witnessing the reality for his sister.

He, too, had personal experience of being a victim of racial violence in Colombo in 1958. He was only thirteen years old. His mother had just had a baby girl, Banu, and he had gone out to buy powdered milk for the child when he saw a mob of Sinhalese beating a Tamil man, and another Tamil man was set alight, burning, screaming for his life, a few yards away on the Galle Road in broad daylight. He had run back home praying to all the Hindu gods and goddesses for safety.

That same night their house was attacked, and they fled next door, to an Anglo Sri Lankan house for safety. The next day they found that their house had been set on fire. They moved to Jaffna as refugees immediately after that.

Since the 1977 general election, many Tamils had had to leave the country for their survival.

'We have to be at the station as soon as possible. We were going to leave today, anyway,' his sister said as she put things in a bag for the journey and hurried the children to get ready.

His niece Sandra changed her long skirt to a gown. She looked different, very simple and beautiful. It seemed like just yesterday that his sister got married and came to Colombo to live with her husband. Param followed them from Jaffna as soon as he entered Colombo University. Within a year little girl Sandra was born. She was a cry-baby, and he'd spent lots of time looking after her while his sister did her housework. Now Sandra was helping his sister do the housework. He smiled at his shy niece, who looked like his sister when she was young.

Then finally, three hours after he had placed the call, the operator called back saying he had a connection to London. Mary sounded so happy to hear from him. 'We missed you on Christmas Day, darling,' she said. 'We heard the news and were so worried, knowing you were on Aeroflot…'

'What news is that?' he asked. 'They didn't tell us anything. We were stranded in Tbilisi for five whole days, and they gave us no explanation.'

'On Monday, Christmas Eve, the Russians invaded Afghanistan to prop up the communist government there.'

'My goodness. Now I understand why they wouldn't tell us anything.'

'They're fighting against the resistance, the mujahideen, who are backed by America. Sri Lanka is siding with America, evidently.'

'And now, I see why we've heard nothing since I arrived here. I guess the Sri Lankan government doesn't want us to know about it.'

He felt too tired to be traveling to Jaffna straight after the six chaotic days in Georgia. But he had no choice, as according to his sister, his father was in the last day or two of his life. Somehow, Param felt his father was waiting to see him.

'You could have brought your wife,' his sister said without looking at him. This was the first time she had mentioned her.

'Father wouldn't like that, would he?' There was no point in talking about Father now, so he stopped mid-sentence.

His sister said, 'He can't say anything, anymore. He stopped talking about two months ago.' She started to cry.

'There's no point in crying,' said her husband, trying to comfort her. Her voice cracked and she started to cry loudly with her children standing nearby, who on seeing their mother's upset also started to cry.

'He worked so hard to bring us up. He never drank, he was never bad to anyone...'

In saying that, Param thought, she was not entirely correct. She knew well that it was because of his father's behaviour that he hadn't come back to Sri Lanka all these years. She may have been thinking, like everyone else, that he was the one who should feel guilty, for marrying a white woman without his father's permission.

'Who lives for ever? We all have to go one day.' This was his brother-in-law's philosophy.

'He is not that old; he is only sixty-five.' She sniffed, her voice sounding strange after all her tears.

His sister was in her late thirties, but she looked much older. Maybe it was because of all the problems they faced causing her so much worry. He felt alienated from it all— his family, his home, his country in turmoil for the last twelve years—yet, he hadn't suffered through it all.

When his sister was ready to leave, he noticed how she had transformed herself into a non-Hindu woman. She had no *thali* around her neck, the special necklace which Hindu women wear when they get married. In place of the thali, she was wearing a simple plastic necklace. Nor did she have a red *pottu*, the red dot on her forehead.

'Don't look at me like that, brother, we have no identity anymore in this country. You can't even walk freely in the country you were born in.'

Both sides of Galle Road in Colombo were full of new buildings and hotels, but not many Tamil shops. Once upon a time Colombo had a large number of Tamil people from Jaffna.

'You see, after the 1977 election, when the Tamil people voted for a separate state, the situation got worse. The government officials were themselves involved in violence against the minority Tamils,' his brother-in-law explained.

Where was democracy? For the people, by the people, of the people, the election should have produced a democratic system. It's all right in theory, but in reality?

But he didn't respond to his brother-in-law. He didn't want to get involved with politics. He wanted to see his father and do whatever he could do for his family and stay far away from everything.

'Sir, what do the Tamils in London say about us and the problems we face here?' the taxi driver asked him politely.

What did Tamils in London say about them? He could not answer that question. He had never been involved in Tamil politics in London. As far as he was concerned, he only cared about his family; he didn't get involved with the emotional, political games played by some so-called community leaders in London.

When he took Mary to Tamil concerts or religious festivals, she felt that she didn't understand the culture or the people. Mary was not a traditional English woman who thought that English culture was superior to everyone else's; and she wanted to understand his traditions and culture.

'Oh well, you don't have to be a specialist on my culture, but I want you to see my people and their culture,' he used to say.

The taxi driver was still awaiting Param's answer. 'They all left the country for a better life as soon as we started to experience problems. Are they all happy there?'

How the hell did he know whether other Sri Lankans who lived in Britain were happy? He laughed and said, 'When Tamils need a job they come from Jaffna to Colombo; now they go to a foreign country. That is simply the search for survival. I don't look any further into their lives than that.'

His niece Sandra looked at her uncle curiously. She didn't remember him, having been a toddler when he left. Now, she was fourteen and trying to learn about the world through her own experience. She'd heard a lot about her uncle. Her mother and aunts still wrote to him and talked to him now and then on the phone.

'Is there no trouble for Tamils in London?' she inquired.

There are lots of problems for black people in general, he wanted to say.

They seemed to think that London was free from all prejudice; one day they would

learn that that is not so.

The station was busy as usual, full of foreign people. He thought about Liz and wished for her to have good time in Sri Lanka.

The train was the same as twelve years ago. People wanted to have corner seats, and comfortable seats; they were arguing for it. Train traders were selling their food products including young coconuts. Young men were making sexual remarks about young women who were alone.

He imagined Liz taking a train like this. She was alone and beautiful. How would she put up with men like these? Param felt disturbed by her innocence which enabled her to talk to everybody. It made him uncomfortable to think of Liz in trouble. But then, he thought, she was clever; she would get to know the customs quickly.

How different she was from Mary. Mary was a bit reserved, studying people first before getting to know them later. Liz would say hello to any stranger, whereas Mary wouldn't unless she were with people she knew.

As the train started to move, his mind wandered from London to Moscow to Colombo and now to Jaffna. The fresh country air made him go to sleep in no time. He was dreaming of many things which were deep in his thoughts.

How would his mother receive him? His father had written to him, telling him that he never wanted to see him again. 'You have gone against our ways, by marrying someone with no understanding of our caste, our tradition and our culture. You are not my son, anymore.'

But the money that he sent to his family was never returned.

Having a male child is like an insurance policy in a Tamil family, he said to himself. He got up now and then, slept a bit, dreaming of the changing scenery around him that day. What a change. Within one day he had seen many nationalities, many faces and heard many different languages.

London was under heavy snow, and Meera was making a snowman in their garden, his wife had told him on the phone. It was so hot on the train to Jaffna that he undid the top button on his shirt.

He bought a coconut, his sister complaining about the price, and drank all the milk. He had only paid a few rupees more than the usual price, but his sister said this trade targeting western tourists was part of the reason for the rising cost of living. There was not much in the way of fish or vegetables for the people who produced them; they had to sell them to expensive hotels who entertained white tourists in order to buy bread and rice for the poor Sri Lankans.

Param couldn't understand his sister's logic. 'If they don't sell their produce, they will starve,' he said.

'No,' she replied, 'the number of people selling fish is increasing because of the markets. Producers of other foods are joining the export market, too, which is making it difficult for people to buy bread.'

He felt sad for the changing situation in Sri Lanka.

The heat made him exceptionally tired. He went to sleep again. He dreamt about London and Moscow again, but suddenly he got up sweating. He looked around, still half asleep, but then realised he was only dreaming. When he looked out of the window, he had the feeling of seeing someone he used to know. He'd thought he saw his former girlfriend, Karthiga.

'Does it snow in London?' his nephew Ravi asked him.

'Yes, it's snowing now, and my daughter is creating a sculpture of a snowman in our garden, my wife said,' he told his nephew.

'What is a snowman?' Ravi asked.

Param explained to him about his daughter's imagination with snow like any other kids in England during the heavy winter. Param was busy looking at the man with the beard who had just jumped onto the next section of the train. He reminded Param of someone who had been very close to him in the past. Some of his friends were in London, some in America, some in other parts of the world, and a few were still left in Sri Lanka. Will I meet any of them? he asked himself.

He lay back and closed his eyes. Again he saw Karthiga. Where would she be? Would she talk to me? Would she curse me? Would she ignore me, would she treat me like the most awful person in the whole world? He didn't want to think anymore. I hope I don't see her at all, he wished.

The noise of Jaffna railway station woke him up. It was busy, as usual. The railway station had been given a new face-lift. Jaffna station was very different from Colombo station. Colombo was a cosmopolitan city where you saw all kinds of people, but here you only saw well-to-do middle-class Tamils coming from Colombo or abroad.

It was very dark when he walked out from the hustle and bustle of the station, and he could hear the noise of the Hindu temple bell. The bells sounded so rhythmic and clear. Jaffna was an extraordinary city, the centre of strong Hindu Tamil idealism, blended with modern, westernised people and their life.

Someone placed an arm on his shoulder and said, 'Hello.'

Param turned to see the man with the beard from the train.

'You... you...'

'Sathyan.' The man with the beard laughed.

Sathyan hadn't changed much, except for his nicely trimmed beard. His sparkling eyes, ever smiling face, and most of all his handsome appearance were all as Param remembered.

'How nice to see you,' Param said to his friend. Sathyan was one of his closest friends when they were young.

'So, you can still speak Tamil,' Sathyan said.

'Yes, I can; my name is still Paramanathan, but I shortened it to Param, as English people do not like long names... believe me, I haven't changed it to Sam or James.' They both laughed.

'Hello, Sathyan.' Param's sister came up to them.

'Where are you living, now?' she enquired, 'I haven't seen you for a long time.'

'I am still in Sri Lanka, working in Kandy. Some of us are left to serve our country, and I'm one of the poor ones who couldn't afford a ticket abroad.'

Param smiled at him happily and stared at his friend for a long time.

'What's the matter, you seem to be measuring me like a tailor about to make a shirt out of my skin,' said Sathyan, still looking at his friend. 'So, when did you arrive?'

'Early this morning.'

'With the family?'

'No, my father is not well, I had to come in a hurry.'

'Oh, I am sorry to hear about your father, how long will you be in Jaffna?'

'I have taken six weeks holiday. I wanted to see you.'

'You know my sister's house at Thinnaveli? Please come.'

'Poor Sathyan.' Param's brother-in-law watched Sathyan disappear into the dark, walking very slowly. 'He lost all his family during the riots in 1977, and his leg was broken. Now he is disabled.'

They took a taxi for Jaffna Hospital from the station.

'Every time there was a riot, we came here and said we would never go to Colombo again. But what could we do? We need a job to survive, we have no choice but to go to places like Colombo and Kandy and risk facing attacks.' His sister was still talking about the riots when they got out of the taxi.

The smell of the hospital made Param feel sick.

'I don't know whether they will let us in,' his sister said when she saw people coming out from the wards. 'Visiting time has finished.'

Her husband looked at his watch.

Param went to the ward sister and asked her permission to see his father. She shouted and said they couldn't let anybody in, now. She was fat and had a loud voice.

'Sorry, sister, but we've come from far away. I mean, I have come all the way from London to visit my father. Please let me see him.'

She looked at him for a minute and said, 'Okay, but don't stay long.'

They rushed to the ward which was filled with coughs and moans mixed with the smell of incontinence and faeces.

His mother was standing near his father and holding his hand. She ran towards Param when she saw him.

'I dreamt last night that you would come today.' Tears ran down her cheeks. She held his hand very tightly. She looked worn out, grey, a worried old woman. 'Twelve years, twelve years,' she mumbled whilst taking him to her father's bedside.

That thin, frail figure was his father?

'Appa.' Param bent down to his father's face. His breathing was irregular, his mouth open, and his eyes were fixed to the ceiling. 'Appa,' Param whispered into his father's ears, holding his hand which was cold and lifeless.

He held his father's hand, feeling full of emotion. He knew then that this could be the last touch his father felt on earth. Param felt extraordinary emotion when the old man's eyes turned slightly towards to him.

'I am sorry if I have upset you.' Param whispered to his father's ear.

So many memories flashed back in a second in Param's mind.

'I planned to come many times, but…' Param wanted to tell his father a lot of things, but something was blocking his throat.

Outside, darkness covered the hospital. The dim lights inside made it seem more melancholy and duller. Somewhere in the temple the bells rang in the same melancholy tone.

Father's breathing was getting slower, as if he were saying goodbye to those around him.

Mother wept. 'He loves you, he waited for you.' The time went as slowly as his father's breathing.

'Give him some milk.'

An old woman brought some milk in a silver bowl with a silver spoon. Still holding his father's hand Param put one spoonful of milk in his father's mouth with the other hand. It stayed in his mouth, with some spilling outside. This man who used to shout at the people around him was now laid out to die like a bundle of used cloths. Now, the gasping breathing was the only movement his father made. His father's breathing became shallower and shallower. The old man fixed Param with his eyes, as his breathing grew fainter, and then stopped.

Param was still holding his father's hand.

His mother's cry split the silence like thunder. 'Oh God, why are you so cruel, you take a part of my life, now. My fate is so awful. Have I created so much bad karma that I have to suffer like this?'

One of their relatives, an old lady, closed his eyes and covered the body with a white sheet.

'He waited for you to come to be with him in his last minute,' the old woman said to Param.

He sat there and stared at the body which was nothing more than a white covered object now, while his mother and sister made the arrangements with the hospital authorities to take the body home.

They carried the body in one car, Param and his mother sitting each side of the dead body and holding it at both sides. The body was still warm. Param cried silently. The others would travel in another car. They started the journey home. Mother was still blaming her karma for the loss of her husband.

Karma. Whatever actions we performed in our previous lives, we receive punishment for them in this life. If we were bad in our last life, we had no choice but to suffer for it, now. That was in Hindu myth. Param didn't believe anything like that. But still, he couldn't explain the feeling when he touched his father. He felt that his father knew that Param was with him. He could tell his father was happy to see him. He felt he had waited for him. Did he forgive him? He didn't want to analyse his emotions.

As soon as they arrived home his two other sisters, Gowry and Banu were at the gate, and when they realised their father was dead, they began wailing and crying. Within half an hour the house was filled with relatives and friends. Some came to pay their respects to the dead man. Some came to see Param whom they hadn't seen for twelve years.

His sisters asked him whether he wanted to eat anything or have a rest, but still they were so noisy, talking and crying. Although his father had had a very serious stroke, they had all hoped their father would live for another few months.

The body rested in the hall. Oil lamps, incense, flowers, prayers all made the situation strongly religious and deeply sad.

Death was very important in Hindu families. The rituals were very complicated and meaningful. Param, being the only son, had to perform all the rituals for his father. Although he hadn't been in touch with these traditions and practices for a long-time, he had to follow the family's wishes.

Only a week ago he was a perfectly happy son who had very little to do with his mother and others, but today he was the important one performing the last rituals for his father.

The moon was nearly full that night, and the sky was full of stars against a clear blue background. He hadn't seen a moon like this in twelve years. London didn't have this special moonlight.

'Anna.' (brother). His youngest sister Banu had been only nine years old when he left home. She was a thin girl with a pigtail and a very sharp tongue, which made everyone cross. She was always their father's favourite pretty little girl, and because she was the youngest in the family, she always got what she wanted. Now she looked so different.

'Banu.' He held her hand in which she held a cup of hot milk and took the cup from her.

'Mm.'

She was crying.

'Appa is gone,' she wept.

'Well, there is nothing we can do,' he said trying to be philosophical.

'Who will take care of us, now?' She sat near him. They were under the mango tree under the beautiful midnight full moon in Jaffna. He realised the duty he had for his family. Banu looked so vulnerable and very sad.

'How about me? I am your brother. I know I haven't been in touch with you all for a long time as I should have, but I never forgot my duty.' He didn't want to try to justify himself. After all, he had sent enough money to build houses for the girls as dowries when they married. And now and then he'd written to his sister in Colombo to get their news.

'How long are you going to stay?' she asked after a while.

'I don't know; it depends on how long Amma wants me to stay. But I cannot stay more than a couple of months.' He felt that his younger sister wanted to tell him something as she was fiddling with the chair. But he had no idea what it was. They needed more time to open up and talk freely.

He knew that his mother would talk to him about his sisters and their marriage prospects. He would have to participate in the process of looking for good husbands for them.

# Chapter 5

The cremation took place the following evening. Param had done his last duty for his father, lighting the fire on his father's pyre; in no time at all huge flames shot up into the moonlit night. He watched the sparks from the fire, wondering whether they contained messages for anyone? Life was a drama with all its chaos, but we all end up as nothing but ash.

His elder sister had to go back to Colombo with her family after a week. Visitors were still coming and going, and his mother and sisters continued to cry every time another relative visited them.

Param wanted to go to Jaffna city centre to look for his friends at the book shops or coffee bars, especially Sathyan, whom he had run into on the train.

He received a letter from Mary, which made him feel happy, and felt the pain of being away from them for the first time. 'It is still snowing in London,' she wrote.

He was still sweating with the heat in Jaffna.

Far away there was *Veena* music from one of houses while he was talking on the phone to Mary in London. The music connected him to his past. It's nothing real, he thought. He is no longer a twenty-three-year-old who was getting ready to go to London. Now, he was talking to his wife many thousands of miles away.

He watched the leaves of palm trees at the back of the house which were swaying to the rhythm of the morning breeze. He heard the kids with their parents, young girls and boys on their bikes going to school along the lanes of Jaffna. He thought about his darling daughter Meera and wanted to get back to London, soon. The beauty of the morning scene in Jaffna was so different from the drizzly, cold in London.

Suddenly, he thought about Liz in Tbilisi just a few days before, at the ancient fort during their tour. Would she like to visit Jaffna? he wondered. The smell of the morning food brought his thoughts back from Tbilisi.

He had a bath and got ready to go into town, and Mother brought him some breakfast. It was so long since he had had his mother's meals. Although she was mourning the loss of her husband, she still made an effort to look after him.

She looked at him proudly while he wasn't looking. 'You should have brought your little daughter.'

'Oh, yes? What about my wife?' he asked her.

'You are the boss of the family now, and you can bring anyone you like.'

'She is not just anyone, she is my wife,' he said firmly. He had stopped smiling, now. There was a silence. She had to learn to accept him as he was. She couldn't go back into the past.

'You should take care of your sisters.'

'I will.'

'So, when are you going back?'

'In five weeks' time.'

There was a lot of noise outside in the garden, where his niece and nephew were having fun with the goats and cows; his second sister Gowry was having a good time with them.

'You must meet the young man we have chosen for Gowry.'

'What?' He had no idea about this and got very annoyed. He was the one sending money for the marriage arrangements, but they never bothered to inform him. He was trying to prove that he was the eldest now and the person who must take responsibility for everything, but...

'It's a good arrangement. Especially as getting a man from London is not...'

'You mean to say you chose someone from London without telling me.'

'Don't get angry. He is on holiday here now, and the proposal came along.' Mother's voice sounded guilty and uncomfortable.

He could tell she felt guilty. It's a bit bloody late for remorse, he wanted to shout. 'Did they come to the funeral?' he asked.

'No, they are in India visiting temples.'

'I see. Praying to God to get lots of money for the dowry, I bet,' he snapped, and got up.

He felt humiliated. All those years he had been sending money to 'buy' a good husband for his sister, but they couldn't be bothered to consult him when the time came to make the deal. He felt like going home to London immediately. Didn't they consider him a part of the family?

'Why are you so angry?' His mother's voice sounded so sad. 'You must see, it's not

easy to find a good man, nowadays.'

'I don't want to see anything.'

'Don't be silly, son. Gowry's horoscope is not that good. Finding the same type...'

'Oh, stop it, Amma.'

'What is the matter?' She was nearly in tears.

'Nothing. If you like it, do it. Get on with it. I am sure you will send me the bill for the expenses.'

He got up, went outside, and put a mat under a mango tree to relax a bit in the heat of the day. He had a plan to go to town to look for his friends, but the news of his sister's betrothal upset him. His elder sister had not told him about this when he landed in Colombo last week. He really could not understand where he stood in the family. Was he only there to provide financial help for them? He was so troubled with all this information just after he'd arrived in Jaffna.

His mother went out into the other side of the garden, where the children were playing with Gowry.

His youngest sister Banu came along with iced tea on a tray. She was twenty-one years old, now, with a slender figure, a pair of beautiful eyes and a smiling face.

'Hey, my little sister.' He pulled her hair softly.
'What?'
'Aren't they arranging anyone for you, yet?' He tried to hide his anger. 'How could they buy a good man for you? No one would come near you if they knew how sharp a tongue you have,' he teased her.

She got the message and smiled at him.

'Why are you smiling, you are not looking for someone?' he asked slowly whilst studying her expression.

Banu looked at him straight and asked: 'Will you help me to get married if I have chosen someone for myself?'

'You are joking, aren't you?' How could a girl from a Jaffna Hindu family talk to her brother like that?

'Oh, Anna.' Her eyes sparkled with joy. 'You look like you've seen a ghost,' she said.

He was still looking at her, the sun rays sneaking through the palm leaves and reflecting in her beautiful big eyes, which always reminded him of a herring fish.

'Well, who is the victim?' he said, trying to laugh, too. 'Oh yes, you are a good Hindu and a Tamil woman who will not reveal her man's name,' he teased her.

'You know him.'

'What? I don't remember anyone here who would take that kind of risk of falling in love with you.'

He was still smiling. Somehow talking to Banu was making him feel better because he felt at least someone was talking to him about the family and what was going on.

'Go on, tell me his name.' He lifted her face up to him. No wonder someone fell in love with these beautiful eyes, he thought.

The chickens were making a lot of noise as Amma put grains out for them. The breeze was as gentle as Banu's words. 'Well, he is… he is…'

'Go on.'

'He is your Karthiga's brother Sabesan.'

His heart nearly stopped for a second.

'What?' He nearly screamed but tried to keep his voice down to avoid his mother and the others hearing him.

Two things shocked him. One was the way she announced the man as 'your Karthiga's brother', 'your Karthiga'. How many people like Banu were still thinking about Param and Karthiga? He'd thought that story was dead and buried.

The other thing was the caste that Sabesan came from. Didn't she know?

'Banu.' His face was pale, and he couldn't face her eyes.

'What, Anna?' Her voice was firm and clear.

'Banu…'

The sunshine was brilliant; there was a call from a man selling fish from the street. He continued, 'Banu, do you know Sabesan's caste? Don't be silly, our family…'

He was breathing heavily. Does she know the consequences of falling in love with a lower caste man in Jaffna? Does she know there that more than thirty percent of Jaffna Tamils are oppressed due their caste and under the brutal control of the upper caste? He was speechless.

She looked at him like a stranger. He wondered whether she in a dream world of love or what? Oh, God, the thinking of new generation is fantastic, but what would his family think?

'I am not silly. I am serious. I'm not going to be a coward like you and give up my love because he... he comes from a different background.' Her voice was sharp.

'We're not talking about my personal life,' he snapped at her. The time when he was asked to obey his father's words had passed, but where was his sister in this new world of modernism and changes?

'Well brother, I have to talk about my personal life. That's all I know. It's easy for you to...' She stopped as soon as she saw their mother and went to the kitchen.

Amma looked at her son. He looked so pale and confused.

Jaffna town was busy as usual. He went to Poobalasingham's, which was a famous book shop in Jaffna where he used to go with his friends a long time ago. Jaffna was not very different from Colombo at present, with hundreds of new buildings and shops. The women were different too as they were wearing more western outfits than when he was here before. In the past it was unusual to see a girl on a bike, or in a mini skirt, but now there were plenty of them.

Changes. Yes, changes are inevitable. When his father found about Param's love for Karthiga, his father very cunningly separated him from his love by sending him to London.

Now, his sister was telling him that she was in love with Karthiga's brother Sabesan, and she seemed determined to marry him.

His mind was restless. He felt lonely and a stranger to the place and the situation. He wished he could run into someone he knew. He wanted to talk to someone he was close to. He suddenly remembered Sathiyan. Param thought Sathiyan might still be in Jaffna and staying at his sister's house.

He went to the bus stop and waited. Wasting time at bus stops was not something Param was familiar with. Many things in Jaffna were familiar, however, such as the cinema posters. They were everywhere: tearful heroines, macho heroes and fat villains with fast cars. He hadn't seen any Tamil films for a long time in London, and he had no intention of starting any new habits, either, as most Tamil cinemas showed nothing but rubbish.

He decided to walk to Sathiyan's sister's house, about two miles away from Jaffna town, passing the bookshop he used to go to on the way. He used to read lots of novels; he rather liked progressive novels. Karthiga, used to read Tamil love stories.

'I wish I could write a novel,' she had told him many times.

He wanted to forget Karthiga. But her name and face kept coming back into his mind. Banu had given him a shock. Why couldn't she have found someone else, anyone else except Karthiga's brother? After all, he hadn't meant to harm anyone. If he could have planned his life with no complications, he would have done so. But there were many things which happened as if they were destined to happen.

He fiddled with the pages of newspapers on a stall.

'Hey, what's going on? Looking for the best-selling Tamil novel?' Param looked up. Sathiyan was standing next to him. Param was so pleased to see him.

'Would you believe it if I told you I was walking to your house, and just stopped to buy a daily?' Param said.

Sathyan looked at his friend who had been walking in the heat and was sweating.

'Come on. Let's have something cool.'

Param and Sathyan went to Subas café where they used to go. A place for college students to go and have laugh and joke while they waited for spicy snacks and sugary tea. Sathyan watched the way Param was spending his money. They had been teenagers and did not have enough money to buy whatever they wanted.

'Don't worry. Compared to my expenses in London, this is nothing,' Param said

as he tasted his passion fruit juice. It seemed his friend could not afford to order what Param was ordering, now.

'Most Tamils went away abroad just to get a better life for themselves,' said Sathyan.

'What else could we have done?' Param replied. He and Sathyan had gone to different universities, but they had graduated at the same time.

'Would you have stayed if you had got a good job?' Sathyan asked him.

'Maybe. How about you?' Param could not say why he was sent away to London by his father. He thought about it for a minute but could not and would not want to bring the subject up, now. He asked the question of Sathyan, instead.

'What about me?'

'What are you doing, what's happening in your life, marriage and family?'

Sathyan finished his juice and snacks and said, 'You see, my dear friend, marriage, women and personal pleasures come easy if you're doing well and climbing the social ladder. But for people like me who have limited choices and resources, marriage and other things are luxuries. But don't think I'm not happy because I'm not married. I have committed myself to other things.'

In part Sathyan was joking, in part he was being philosophical. Param's sister had mentioned that Sathyan's family had suffered a great deal due to the communal violence in 1977.

'What are you doing now?' They both came out of the café, where there was a torn poster of the socialist party on the broken wall. They had belonged to a progressive circle when they were students. The posters were a metaphor of the decaying progressive ideologies in Jaffna since Tamil nationalism had been carefully planted by the traditionalists.

'Well, nothing big, working as a clerical servant in Kandy.'

When Sathyan mentioned Kandy, Param remembered Liz. What would she be doing now? He wondered for a moment.

'How about the family? My sister told me that your family had a hard time.'

'My parents were both killed by the mobs. The house was destroyed. My leg was broken. Still, at times, I can't believe that I'm still alive.'

'I am sorry to hear that.'

They walked away from the café.

'What do you think will happen to the Tamils?' Param asked his friend.

'What do you mean?'

'What I mean is, I believe that it is because of our leaders' lack of understanding of the whole political situation regarding the Tamils that we are in this position.'

'Be careful what you say, Param. This is not London. It's easy for people to pass remarks if they're not the ones getting hurt.'

Neither of them said much more until they came to a lane where there were not many people around.

But it seemed Sathyan agreed with Param's statement. 'You see, here there is no law and order,' he commented. 'The rulers who are supposed to care for the people are not doing so; instead of making the country a better place, this so-called democratic government is treating people like animals. You don't know how many people I know who have disappeared, you can't imagine the torture their families go through when a young Tamil gets arrested by the Sinhalese government.'

They arrived at Sathyan's sister's place, which seemed calm and cool because of the trees around the house.

'Yes, I don't know everything that's happening in Sri Lanka,' said Sathyan, 'but as far as I can see there is drama everywhere. That's the problem. Tamils abroad live in a fantasy world wishing they could go back maybe two thousand years when they had their glory and wealth.' Sathyan changed into his sarong.

'Well, when a nation faces oppression, its people always go back or look for things which make them feel good.' Param responded.

'Nobody is denying that Tamils are oppressed by the majority government in Sri Lanka, but the solution is not to ask for more trouble, the solution has to have reasonable and justifiable politics,' said Sathyan.

'Well, well, look who is home,' said Sathyan's sister as she came in from shopping. 'Sathyan told me you were in Jaffna.'

Sathyan's family were honest people. His father had been an English teacher, who had introduced Sathyan to progressive thinking, talking about the great poets and writers in the world.

Sathyan's sister was a teacher, too. She didn't have a *thali*, the holy chain of a married woman, around her neck. She noticed that Param was looking for it.

'Oh, Param, you don't have to ask questions. I am one of the Tamil women who lost her husband at the hands of…' She couldn't complete her sentence.

She went into the kitchen. He knew that she was crying, and he didn't want to upset her by asking more questions.

He followed Sathyan to the well where he was having a bath.

'You need to bathe three or four times a day in Sri Lanka. How are you managing the heat?'

'Well, the heat outside is tolerable compared to the heat from my family,' he joked.

'What, are they still talking about you marrying a white woman?'

'Oh no, not only that.'

'So, what else is the matter?'

Sathyan was still pouring cold water over himself, and Param started pouring his heart out to his friend about everything going on in his family.

'Banu is in love with a young man called Sabesan.' Param didn't want to mention Karthiga's name.

'You mean the poet Sabesan?'

'I don't know whether he writes poems or what. I only know he teaches at the tutory.'

'Yes, that's the one, the poet Sabesan. I thought so. I saw them once at the theatre.'

'You saw them at the theatre?' So Hindu Tamil girls in Jaffna had the courage to go to the cinema with their boyfriends, now.

'Param, things have changed a lot. Anyway, what is wrong with them being together if they are in love?'

'There is nothing wrong with being in love, but can't you see how my family is going to react?'

'Param, I don't know whether your family will react against the relationship or not, but I'll tell you your future brother-in-law has made lots of trouble for the police force, already. So, he needs to be very careful.'

'What are you saying?'

'I am saying that your sister is not in love with an ordinary fellow. Sabesan is a revolutionary. He supports the armed struggle for Tamils.' Then he looked at Param curiously.

'What is the matter? Why are you looking at me like that?' Param asked Sathyan.

'I didn't realise, when you were attacking the Tamil leaders like that, that you were a militant supporter.'

'Oh no, I'm not a militant supporter, but of course I support peace and freedom and justice for Tamils,' Param said quickly.

'Well, your brother-in-law to be will give you more lectures on the subject, I believe.' Sathyan said with a smile.

'I don't want to talk politics. What am I going to do about Banu's problem?'

'Listen to me, my friend. There is nothing without politics. If Sabesan is now a militant, it is because of what happened to his family. Men are not saints, they have feelings, too. Although I am against action without political analysis, I cannot blame the young Tamil men who have sought a military solution to defend us from the barbarism of state terrorism.'

Sathyan finished bathing. 'What happened to his family?' Param's voice was almost trembling. God, please don't tell me that Karthiga is dead, too, he prayed, even though he didn't believe in God.

Sathyan didn't answer.

'You'd better ask Sabesan.' Sathyan said abruptly as he didn't want to continue further.

The two old friends sat down to the vegetarian meal which Sathyan's widowed sister had prepared for them.

'Your sister said that she lost her husband, too. Was it a government murder?'

'No. Her husband was killed by Tamil Tigers. They killed anyone whom they thought was a danger to their work.'

Param was feeling shock after shock since he came from London to what seemed like another planet. The Jaffna he knew when he left in 1968 was no longer there. Talking, walking, living seemed to be a dangerous matter, unless one says 'yes' to Tamil nationalism.

He wanted to talk to Banu, to know more about Sabesan, his writings and his involvement with politics. It seems there were a few groups started to formulate here in order to have a 'separate state for Tamils'. He also wanted to ask her whether she agreed with Sabesan and his way of thinking. But their house was always full of visitors.

He was reluctant to get involved in the political situation, which was very complicated and dangerous. He wanted to go home to London as soon as possible, but at the same time he couldn't resist feeling that he should advise Banu about her future. Love is one thing which no one has any control over; how much did she know about the complexity of it?

He got a letter from Mary, and after reading it he felt he wasn't close to his mother and sister the way he used to be. They seemed to be in a world ruled by ideology of the past.

Suddenly, he felt he was in a place where all seemed messy and fearful. He wanted to go home to London from Jaffna and see Mary and Meera, but he had to wait until the thirty-first day after his father's death. He felt he was a stranger to his sisters, now. The years of separation had made them very different from one another.

That morning when his niece and nephew were at their grandparents, Gowry was at school and Mother was up at the hospital for her appointment with the woman next door, he went out to the market to buy some fruits and think things over.

When he came home, Banu was busy making a meal alone in the kitchen. She seemed to be doing things in her own way with not much help from anyone. He admired her energy, independence, most of all her determination to get what she wants in her future. She was good at many things, including finding a partner.

He sat on the stool near the kitchen door. She was having trouble with the oil cooker. He was reluctant to begin discussing the subject of Sabesan. What would he say if she said that her love affair with Sabesan had nothing to do with him at all?

'What are you thinking?' Banu questioned him while trying to light the cooker.

'Nothing much.'

'I'd love to meet your little girl,' she said.

'You will soon.'

She did not say that she wanted to meet his wife, too.

'My wife will be happy to meet you all, too, you know.'

She knew the meaning of his remarks; none of them ever asked about Mary. 'How will she react to having us as her in-laws?'

'What do you mean?'

'Well she is not our type.' She said without looking at him. Banu started to scrape the coconut.

'Yes, she is not our type, but then none of us are the same as others; she has her way of living and I have mine, we're happy together. That's the main thing in love and marriage, give and take, trying to understand each other.'

She began to see that he wanted to talk about Sabesan. She went outside and put down the used coconut flakes for the chickens to eat. He felt that she did not want to talk about his life in London.

He went to his room and took out Mary's letter and looked at it lovingly. His daughter had sent him a drawing of an elephant.

He didn't have many problems being a happily married man. Mary and he respected and were very fond of each other. Their marriage had been unexpected and sudden; neither of their families had given them their blessing, but that hadn't stopped them.

Mary's family in Dorset hadn't liked their only daughter getting involved with a 'coloured' man. But in UK at that time, many young people were determined to have their own lives, and Mary was no different. Mary's family got used to her being married to Param after a while, and her mother had grown very fond of Meera, the only granddaughter she had.

Param enjoyed his life as an ordinary man, comfortably well off. But subconsciously he suffered from guilt about his past, as he had abandoned Karthiga's love. He knew that there was nothing he could do about it, but the pain in his heart was still there.

He hadn't come back to the woman he loved in Sri Lanka.

He often felt that he let circumstances call the tune rather than controlling the situation. And sometimes he wondered whether, if he were back in Sri Lanka after his studies and had not met Mary, he would have married Karthiga, because he knew what kind of problems he would have had to face with his old-fashioned family. He thought memories of her had died in his mind, but Banu was now bringing them all to life again. Would Banu understand the problems involved in being with a man from a different caste?

Banu was getting ready to do the washing as he finished bathing in the well. After bathing he sat on the cement stone steps near the well, watching his sister soaping the clothes. Women in Jaffna had not seen washing machines, yet; they spent most of their lives washing and cleaning.

'Why are you watching me, Anna?' she asked her brother, who was sitting next to her. It was one of those beautiful late mornings, with less heat and more breeze.

'Do you know about Sabesan's political activity?' He helped her to put the clothes in other containers to soak. She raised her face and kept the question in her expression, without asking him.

'What do you want me to know?' she asked.

'I heard he had some trouble with the police.'

'It's not only Sabesan; there are lots of young Tamil men who have trouble with the police. He is not a criminal; he writes and speaks about our people's rights. You can't expect us all to be silent while they treat us like dirt.' She continued to soap the clothes.

How could he explain anything to this young woman, in love with a revolutionary? She obviously worshipped him. Banu was a girl from a very strict Hindu family and with an outdated ideology of how one can live as an independent person rather than follow the rule of tradition and be imprisoned in it. She seemed brave to be in love with Sabesan who wanted to change Tamil society.

He understood the anger of Tamils against the Sri Lankan government because of the oppression they had faced for many years. People like Sabesan were more militant than traditional Tamil leaders because most of the leaders, with their English educations, didn't do much for the ordinary Tamil people. But how could people like Sabesan and his friends think they could win a war against the state with just a few young men?

'Don't you worry that he might be destroyed by the police or the army?' He poured more water in the bucket for her to wash the dirty clothes.

He was hearing from his Sinhalese friends in London and remembered what they said to him. March 1971 when the Sinhala leftist organisation the Janatha Vimukthi Peramuna (JVP) took arms against the Sri Lankan government. Then the Prime Minister of Sri Lanka Mrs. Sirimavo Bandaranaike asked the Indian Prime Minister Mrs. Indira Gandhi's help to put down the uprising by the revolutionary Sinhalese youths. Within a few months, not only the revolutionaries but also thousands of ordinary Sinhala people had perished in the name of 'wiping out the leftists'.

Now, the Tamils were taking arms against the Sri Lankan government, which was supported mainly by the Western world.

His beautiful young sister, Banu, looked up and smiled sadly, then said very clearly, 'My dear brother, listen. Do we have any other choice than to fight for our freedom?'

'I thought you studied maths at the tutory,' he said. 'I didn't know you had become the Rosa Luxembourg of Jaffna to talk about changing society.'

She hadn't heard of Rosa Luxembourg. Nevertheless, she believed, 'Nobody has to teach us what to do. What would you do if the army and the police came and killed your family? Wouldn't you fight back?'

'I can't simply say what you should do or anything like that. But he sounds like a bit of an anarchist, emotional rather than political not a revolutionary.'

'Maybe he is emotional, but you didn't go through what he went through in 1977.

You didn't have to face your own...' She stopped washing the clothes, and she buried her head between her knees and suddenly started to cry.

He put his hand on her head and stop the conversation as he did not want to get upset. Everything was just news until you faced it personally.

He had watched the riots in Sri Lanka in London as news, but they were real life for Banu. She could not split herself off from this reality. A turning point in life for someone is not always shared by others or influenced by other's points of view. Experiences in our lives can create or shape us. If Banu were so different from other Tamil women, it might be because she was involved with issues which were making her like that. Still, Param didn't think Sabesan understood what could happen to him in the long run, being involved in Sri Lankan politics.

'Banu, do you think you two will have an easy time if you tell the family about your love?'

'Who is expecting an easy path in life? I'm not,' she replied.

She was so different from the way he remembered her. His little sister Banu had matured in many ways. 'Do you really believe in the ambitions of people like Sabesan? Do you believe we can win over the Sri Lankan government through armed struggle?' he asked her.

'There is nothing in the world a man cannot change or transform. I believe we all have to do something for our own future, rather than sitting around criticising anyone who's daring to do something for other people.'

She can talk, he thought. Oh yes, she can talk very well with no one's help.

'Sabesan is a good teacher, I hear,' he said jokingly.

'No one has to be taught. People learn things through their experience.' Banu was very quick with her words, like Liz Baker.

'Maybe you are right, I might be a militant if I lived here.' He got up to go.

'You would. Definitely, you would, if you had to face what Sabesan had to face.' She got up to put the clothes on the line.

'Does anyone in the family know about your love?'

'Not all of them. But I told Appa the night before he had a stroke.'

She didn't see his face change colour as she mentioned this.

'What?' He tried his best to keep the voice normal.

'I said, I told Appa about Sabesan and me on the day before he had a stroke.'

Param froze for a minute. Suddenly, he wondered if part of the reason for his father's stroke were the shock of hearing about Banu's love affair. He sat back again on the cement floor around the well and looked up at the sky, a clean sky and very hot, indeed.

'What is the matter?' she asked him.

'Nothing,' he said. What was the point of making Banu sad, guilty and unhappy by suggesting that Appa's stroke might have been her fault? The shock of hearing her love for Sabesan, brother of Karthiga, might have stopped his father in his tracks.

Father sent Param to London to split him from Karthiga, but he could not do that to Banu, because he was too old to stand firm against his favourite little daughter.

Or was Banu just a girl in love with a revolutionary?

His mother always put the blame on karma and destiny, that 'whatever you do to others you face the consequences and you must pay for them. If you hurt someone, the mighty will give you pain and hurt one way or another.'

Had denial of Param's love for the girl from another caste brought a punishment of death to his father by hearing of Banu's love with a lower-caste man?

Param sat in his room for a while, thinking about his situation. He was now head of the family. His father wouldn't accept Param's love for Karthiga because she was not in their caste, but he would help Banu to marry Sabesan. Sabesan believed and fought for equality for everyone in the world regardless of whether they belonged to a different caste, class, race or religion. But Sabesan's politics made it dangerous for them to be in Sri Lanka. Would they listen to him and come to England?

# Chapter 6

His mother had been nagging Param for the last few days to go and meet the man who was supposed to marry his second sister Gowry. At the same time, Banu told him, he could go into Colombo and meet her boyfriend Sabesan.

He never thought that he would get into these situations when he was arranging to come to Jaffna. Suddenly, he had to fulfil the duties of the man of the house. They all wanted to do what they thought was right, but he was the one who had to mediate between everyone's differences.

'Will you please go and see Sabesan?' Banu asked him. 'He is staying with his sister in Colombo.'

Banu looked into Param's eyes carefully as she said this. Param felt a lump in his throat. His sister. His sister, Karthiga. Once upon a time that name had made Param dream of heaven. That name had meant the world to him. The person called Karthiga was not just Sabesan's sister. She was, she was…

Param held his feelings inside, not allowing them to spill through in his speech or expression. Already Banu had made a few remarks about Karthiga and him, which he didn't like.

Param had no intention of keeping going the dialogue about the past. He tried to put it out of his mind, but memories of the past were coming to the fore.

Once upon a time, he went to Nallur Hindu temple like any other young man in Jaffna town. That night had been a beautiful evening for a celebration, and the temple was filled with people from all over the district. Most young men were there to look for girls and to make fun of them.

She was there, too, like hundreds of other Hindu girls with silk saris and jewels.

'Let us go, please.' There was a soft voice from near the young woman. He turned and met her eyes. She just looked at him in order to clear their way forward, and their two pairs of eyes stopped, and they looked at each other for a minute or two. Then the girls vanished.

Her image stayed in his thoughts and heart from that minute. She must have been eighteen, a slim girl, shyness spread on her face. He felt the sudden electricity flow in his body when their eyes met. Unknown experience, an extraordinary pleasure and urge to see her more.

The next day he went to the temple to look for her. He could remember the blue sari with the red border she had worn, and he remembered the style of her blouse. He closed his eyes and tried to keep her image in his mind. Soon, he realised he had suddenly become religious and was going to Nallur Temple every Friday.

His friends started to make fun of him, calling him a dreamer, dreaming about the girl, even though he didn't know her name or where she lives lived or what school she was attending.

He lived with her memory in his dreams for a month or so until he got ready to start university. His father had urged him to take extra tuition in maths, so he sought and found a good maths tutor.

Param, a handsome young teenager, rode his bicycle down the lane to the teacher's house. The gate was half opened and one or two goats were running between the houses. And there she was, the girl from the temple, chasing a goat.

After that, many months went by with no words exchanged between them, just a stolen smile now and then. It took all his determination to get to know her, understand her, care for her and love her. He wrote down all his dreams in a letter to her, without knowing whether she would reply or not. He composed it carefully, making ten or twelve drafts.

He took it with him when he went for tuition as usual, hiding the letter inside a book. There was *veena* music coming from the house. He motioned to her brother Sabesan, a small boy of ten, who was playing cricket with his friends. They were obviously not rich with seven children to support on a tutor's wages. But Sabesan was a very bright and happy boy, which might have been because there were only two boys but five girls in the family.

Param asked Sabesan to give the book to his sister Karthiga. Param's heart was pounding with fear, worried in case she might give his love letter to her father. That day he was useless at his lessons, his mind was so full of worries about what Karthiga might think or say.

Finally a few days later as he got ready to go home, she came out of the house with a big smile on her face. She didn't have to put anything in writing.

There wasn't anywhere in Jaffna they could talk or meet often. But within a few months they both entered university. Their love flourished, on Colombo beaches, in student hostels. Victoria Park witnessed their love. He thought that he was the luckiest man in the world to have Karthiga's love.

She was beautiful as well as intelligent. She wrote poems, and he read them. He would bring her western novels, and she would talk about the great epics, *Ramayana* and *Mahabharata*. She would talk about *Ramayana* in order to point out Sita's virtues and chastity. He would say it's up to her to read carefully to understand the message regarding the women in it.

Karthiga was traditional and old fashioned in many ways. She wasn't any different from the other Tamil girls who were undergraduates at the university. She wouldn't let him take her out at night, so they would go to the cinema or the beach in the afternoon, and before it got dark, she would look at the time and say, 'I must get back to the hostel.'

He wanted to scream with frustration, he wanted to spend more time with her, and… and he wanted to make love to her, but she would say that it is not right for women to be with a man before they are married. She was so serious about it that for a long time she wouldn't even let him touch her. She simply said, 'We should wait.'

He tried to talk to her about understanding love, rather than accepting it in the traditional way. 'Love is between two people not between two families, or anybody else,' he used to say. She would listen to him, but never crossed the line of the boundaries she had set.

'Lovers should respect each other's wishes. You must respect what I say, and I will respect what you say,' she would say whilst munching roasted chickpeas.

They spent almost every weekend going to visit ancient palaces and beauty spots. Most evenings they would walk along the Colombo beach or Victoria Park, all the while looking around, just in case they might be seen by any relatives or friends from Jaffna.

When he told her that his father wanted him to go to England to do further study, she was stunned.

'What is the matter?' He lifted her face to see her eyes. She was crying. It was a beautiful evening on Colombo beach, the sun setting under the sea, and there were few people about. He wanted to hold her tight and kiss her, but as usual she wouldn't let him.

'What is the matter?' he wiped her tears.

'I don't want you to go,' she whispered in his ear.

'I don't want to go, either.'

'Then, don't go.'

She looked at the sunset as the beach grew dark. He held her body close to his, and she didn't refuse his touch. It seemed as if she were paralysed. She sat there for a long time staring at the darkening sky.

'Please say something,' he whispered.

She buried her face on his chest and cried for a long time. 'I will pray to God to send you back to me.'

'I will be back,' he promised.

'You wouldn't go with any girls there, would you?'

'No... I will never touch anyone except you.'

'They say London changes people.'

'I'm not someone who has a weak mind, I'm the man who wants to marry you, not any other person on earth.' He kissed her passionately.

'I'll wait for you,' she said.

Nallur Temple, the stolen smiles, the playful arguments about *Ramayana*, evenings on Colombo beach, that passionate kiss against the darkening sky—how could he forget all those things?

# Chapter 7

His father had told him. 'You have to do your duty to your sisters before you think about yourself.' Indirectly his father was warning him not to entertain any idea of enjoying his love with the lower-caste girl. Param had to obey and complete his duty.

He entered a university in London. From a middle-class background, born and brought up mostly in Colombo, Param didn't have difficulty finding people in London with similar interests. Within a few days he began to enjoy London life with his friends, despite the unfriendly weather. He wrote to Karthiga about the cold weather and told her that he needed her to keep him warm.

He studied hard to get his degree, and in the meantime, he got to know people who were interested in third world politics. The whole of Europe was in turmoil in the late 1960s with student marches and rallies against educational changes and other political issues. Playing Beatles music and discussing peace and progressive politics was the main activity for students. Param was inspired by the student activities and political ferment in London. Women were out on the streets, too, to protest against their oppression.

The more he went to student meetings and parties, the less he wrote to Karthiga.

When he had landed in London, he could think of nothing but home and Karthiga; he used to write every night. Being lonely and seeing such a completely different life altogether made him realise how much he loved and wanted to be with her, and he wished she were in London with him.

She was teaching in Colombo and staying with some friends at that time, and he didn't have to worry about pouring his heart out to her. Her friends knew about their love. He wrote very long letters every night for a few months. He wrote many things he wouldn't dream of telling her in person. Somehow London changed him into someone different from the Param who had come from Sri Lanka with few ambitions in life; he became a modern man with modern ideas.

A simple human mind didn't have the strength to stay 'holy' in this land of many distractions. Life seemed to hold contradictions and temptations in every area of London. Instead of wanting to design his life and future in 'traditional' ways, circumstances changed him, giving him new ways and views. Then he wrote every week.

Nearly two years went by. He was going to finish his studies and would be home soon. In his time there, he had made other friends, among whom was Mary, a beautiful white girl who saved his life from the racist attack. She had helped him settle in at university, from finding him a good place to live in Islington to bringing him to progressive and political meetings. Time and the situation were no longer under his control. The place and this girl were more pleasurable than writing letters making promises to a woman many thousands of miles away.

With graduation on the horizon, he learned that he was going to be a father. He looked at his close friend Mary, who was carrying his child. He just didn't know what to say. She understood his feeling. He may have thought girls in London were very careful about unwanted pregnancy.

She talked to him a lot about the pregnancy and her feelings about it. Then said, 'Sorry. I like children, but I am young and after finishing my studies I wanted to do more. I have to tell you that I may get rid of it, but I thought I should tell you first.' She was only twenty-three, enjoying beautiful London life.

She knew he wanted to go home as soon as the study was completed. She would get rid of the foetus as soon as possible if he agreed. Was she doing it for me? Or as she said, 'I do not want to bring up a bastard child.'

That means, she wants him to be part of it if she decides to keep it? He was confused. He thought they were in a situation of turmoil. The young girl who saved his life was telling him that she may get rid of his child inside her.

He had a confused battle with his mind and thoughts. He was twenty-five and did not really understand the changing social and sexual attitudes of the youth as living as you pleased. Or was he behaving according to his upbringing, the old way of 'do not harm others. Just manage your own mind and behaviour'?

'Please go and see Sabesan. He's staying with his sister,' Banu had said. Param was on his way to Colombo to meet Karthiga, sweating with nervous worry. Oh God, he thought, how can I say hello to the woman who said, 'I will wait for you forever, and I will love you until I die?'

Would she understand what happened to me in London? Or would she curse me and tell me to go to hell?

The Jaffna to Colombo train was slow that day, and he was irritable and anxious with guilt. He let his eyes wander out of the window. The forests he used to remember between Jaffna and Colombo were disappearing, and there were new settlements, new buildings and new faces. Paddy fields had been replaced by tobacco and sugarcane for the multi-national companies of western capitalists.

When he got out of the station in Colombo, he remembered the time he came with Karthiga; they'd travelled from Jaffna in different compartments and met at the station. She had smiled at him. She was with her father, his tuition master. He had ceased his private tuition since taking the university entrance examination. The old man told him that his daughter was starting university, too. Param had replied, 'I am glad.'

'It's nice to know that you are entering the university, too,' his old tuition master had said. He seemed not to notice that his daughter smiled at his old student meaningfully.

Many years later, now he was travelling from Jaffna alone. It was a hot day when he arrived at the station, full of these memories. He was reluctant to go and see Sabesan alone. He wished he had come with Sathyan. He felt that going with Sathyan might make the meeting more casual and less emotional between him and Karthiga, as well as with Sabesan.

So he set off for Ratmalana, a suburb of Colombo, where Sathy lived, one of the newly developed areas around Colombo, where many Tamils had been massacred during the 1977 riots. When Param got off the bus he hesitated for a moment, looking around to make sure he had come to the right place. He couldn't speak much Sinhalese, and with difficulty he asked his way to Sathyan's house. An old Sinhalese man showed him the lane to the house.

Param couldn't believe the state of the house. It had been nearly destroyed by fire, and there were other partly damaged houses around the lake at Ratmalana. Sathyan's house used to be a happy house with lots of people. Sathyan's father Rajaram had been a clerical servant and a religious man, an orthodox Hindu who passionately loved Indian classical music. He was always mumbling some tune. He was also partially blind.

Param's sister told him that Sathyan's family had been massacred by Sinhalese racists during the 1977 riots.

Param stood in front of his house and felt sad and angry at the same time. How could anyone burn that old man who never harmed anyone?

'Oy, what are you staring at? These are the leftovers from the Sinhala racist barbarians. Like me, there are many disabled but surviving, come in.' Sathyan came out wearing his charming smile.

Param looked at his friend's face, remembering the BBC World Service programme about the Sri Lankan race riots.

'What's the matter?' Sathyan realised what was going through Param's mind.

'I can't believe this. Why did they have to destroy everything like this?'

'People destroy what they are scared of. For the Sinhalese, they think the Tamils are the enemy; they think they can eliminate the Tamil nation by killing innocent Tamils.'

'Oh, God, Sathyan, I never thought that Sri Lanka could see such barbarism.'

'There are lots of things happening here that you wouldn't want to know.'

They both entered the house. It was nearly empty.

'I don't know whether I should call myself lucky by staying in London away from all this.'

'I would say you are lucky, but as for me, I'll never run away from Sri Lanka.'

'Why not?'

'You don't feel like home. It's not your real home in London, is it?'

'I suppose not, but it's better than living here with the constant fear of riots and murder.'

'Some of us have to live with it. Do you think hundreds of thousands of Tamils can run away?'

'So, what's the solution?'

'Violence must end one day, there is nothing without end,' he said.

'God, help the Tamil people,' Param said reverently.

'You should wish that for all the people in Sri Lanka,' said Sathyan. 'Anyway, let's stop talking about these upsetting matters. How is your family?' Sathyan poured some ginger beer for Param.

'Which one? The family in England seem okay, but the family in Jaffna is giving me headaches.' Param drank the ginger beer.

'What's the problem?'

Param told him that he was in Colombo to see Sabesan, and he said, 'I would be very happy if you would come with me to meet Sabesan.'

'What?' Sathyan stared at his friend.

'Don't look at me like that, Sathyan. I'm afraid I won't be able to talk to Sabesan on my own.' The words spilled from Param like fireworks; he was sweating but not because of the hot weather outside.

Sathyan stayed silent for a few minutes then looked at his friend sympathetically and said, 'I think this is your family matter, and you should go and see him by yourself.'

'This is my family matter, and don't I know it. But...'

'But what?'

Partly, Param didn't want to get into any political arguments with Sabesan. Partly, he didn't want to see Karthiga, and he was afraid to be in a situation where he was alone with her.

He could not remember how much Sathyan knew of their story as they were in two different universities. And if he did know, would Sathyan understand how serious this proposed meeting was to him, especially after the serious tragedies his own family had suffered? Sathyan was a realistic person. Whatever had happened in the past was past. That was his philosophy.

'There is no need to dig one's own grave,' he would say.

'Param, sometimes, whether we like it or not, we have to face things. You should go and talk to Sabesan yourself. I think that would be the best. I don't think Sabesan would want to discuss his relationship with Banu whilst I am with you.'

There was no point in pushing Sathyan. Param had to face Karthiga on his own. There was no question about it.

At his sister's house that afternoon he felt uneasy. He didn't want to talk to his sister and her husband, so he stayed moody and silent. His elder sister Geetha thought it was because he hadn't got a telephone call from Mary in London. She asked him to come with her to see the second sister Gowry's future husband who was staying only a few miles away from their house in Colombo. Now, he had to play the elder son and go and meet Gowry's fiancé.

Gowry's fiancé, Mahadeva was a plump looking man with hazy eyes and an artificial smile on his face. He was an engineer in London, he told Param.

Mahadeva had arranged the marriage from London, yet no one had bothered to tell Param.

'I am sorry that we couldn't inform you of our engagement. We didn't think you would be coming to Sri Lanka.'

Mahadeva voice was somewhat sarcastic, that's for sure. He wasn't really sorry for anything. Param could sense that.

Mahadeva's sister went on and on about her wonderful brother who was still keeping up the traditions and values of a Hindu man instead of getting involved in undesirable relationships. He knew what she was hinting at.

'There are not many men coming home to get married among their own kind, you know? Of course, I don't mean…'

Mahadeva's sister stopped when Param looked at her sharply. He disliked the family immediately for making the assumption that he was a bad man because he had married a white woman instead of coming home to marry his 'own kind'. He wanted to get out of their house as soon as possible. He couldn't stand their talk of traditions and values, yet they openly talked about the 'price' for the groom. Mahadeva's sister said that they'd had plenty of proposals with excellent dowries but they chose Gowry because they thought she was an obedient and nice girl.

'What do you think?' His sister Geetha asked him on the way home.

'What's the point of saying anything, now?'

'He is a good match,' Param's sister had told him earlier.

To which Param had replied angrily, 'Oh yes, he has to be, otherwise, it's no good paying him such a big dowry.'

He hated men who put a price on themselves.

They talked about getting Gowry to London. Mahadeva would be going back to London soon, but Gowry would have to wait until the funeral rituals finished in a couple of weeks' time.

On his way home he thought about his family; his relationship with them had more to do with traditional beliefs than with close emotional ties. He had come to Jaffna because he was the son and eldest in the family, and he had to go and see Gowry's future husband because he was the one who had to disburse the dowry. He also had to go and see Sabesan because Banu expected her elder brother to take care of her.

Had they discussed anything with him and his family in London up to now? Certainly not. No one could blame his father for dying, no one could blame his mother for hurrying up Gowry's marriage, and no one could say anything if Banu wanted to choose her own husband.

There was one month left of his holiday, and the responsibilities he had to face during that time were tremendous. Like it or not, he had to sort out some of these things. He didn't like the way Mahadeva was rushing his family into a quick marriage. With all the proposals going back and forth during the last few months, Mahadeva had never bothered to get in touch with Param. And they had both been in London—so he'd have been easily contactable.

Perhaps he found out that Param was married to a white woman and had not many family ties in Jaffna. Or maybe, for whatever reason, Mahadeva didn't want Param to have the chance to know him before he married Gowry. More and more these days, Tamil marriages were becoming a commercial exchange with money and gifts. Why did relationships have to be based on selfishness? Would Gowry love this Mahadeva person and live happily ever after?

What should I do about Banu's love affair? he asked himself.

Should he tell his elder sister in Colombo about Banu? Would he have to see Sabesan? Someone might find out that Param was going to meet Sabesan and inform his sister? What would Param say if his sister asked about him meeting Sabesan? Would the family ever accept Sabesan as a family member? Sabesan came from a different caste. So that made Banu's love affair difficult to sort out in the normal way.

Param walked to Dehiwela from Kollupitiya, a very long walk. There were so many people in Galle Road, yet he felt lonely walking alone in Colombo. He had a strong urge to be in Islington cuddling his daughter and embracing his wife.

The family he had come from seemed split apart from him. The family he had met and made seemed so real and loving. He loved Mary, as a friend, as a companion and as a good wife. But he had never told her about his past. When they got married, they both agreed that neither would talk about the past unless they had some important things to say.

He didn't have much in his past except Karthiga and his love for her. But he had decided to keep it to himself. Mary has nothing to do with it, he thought.

Mary didn't say much about her past, either; she said, 'Whatever happened in the past is just the past. It has nothing to do with my life with you.'

But when Mary said that she was going to have a baby he was shocked. He had never considered that it would happen to him. He had still planned to finish his study as soon as possible and return to Ceylon and marry Karthiga, but that hadn't stopped him from having a good time in London, although he had promised Karthiga that he wouldn't touch any girl in London.

He wasn't an old fashioned, traditional Tamil boy in any sense. He had broken the Hindu caste barrier by falling in love with Karthiga, and he had been determined to marry her after fulfilling his duty to his family.

He had never wanted to stay in England. He didn't like the cold. He didn't like most of the people's attitudes. He had arrived in September. Getting used to the people, the environment, it was all too much, just before Christmas, when London was filled with snow and overcoats. He had never imagined that people could seem so difficult to get know and be friendly with. He thought that the weather might be partly to blame. He thought about Karthiga nearly all the time. He remembered her smile, her cry, her laugh, her cuddles and especially that passionate kiss on the beach.

Mary was a friendly first year student. For a while he liked her just as any other friend. But she was more than any other friend, helpful, kind. But most of all the more she liked him the more he liked her.

He walked along the river Thames for a long time thinking, just after Mary had told him that she was going to have his child. He'd always assumed that women in England would be careful and never forget to use birth control. Mary told him that she would abort the child if he thought it was too much responsibility and that he should not feel guilty about it; she didn't want to see him upset.

It was too much for him to take in. In Sri Lanka they said that a woman would be thought of as a virgin forever as long as she didn't get pregnant before marriage, but that didn't apply to men.

He felt extremely upset thinking about Mary having an abortion. He could never be part of any sort of killing. To accept Mary's abortion would be like authorising a murder. The girl who saved his life, now prepared to have an abortion as she did not want him to change his plans to go back home. He cried for the first time in a long time. He knew that he couldn't let Mary have an abortion, and he never wanted to abandon Mary with his child.

Param would never be able to marry Karthiga.

He thought about the situation he was in in London. He was going to be a father without being married to the woman who was carrying his child in her. He knew that his promises to Karthiga had to be deleted from his thoughts to save his child. He knew he would never forgive himself for breaking his promise to Karthiga in Ceylon, but he did not know any other way.

He went to the registry office with Mary for their hasty marriage and signed the papers declaring that he was now a married man. He wrote to his father very simply that he had got married to an English woman; that's all.

Param's father was not only an arrogant man regarding the caste system; he was also a cunning person in calculating his children's future. He thought that having only one son in the family was a sad thing, because the expectations on the son of a Tamil Hindu family are so strong.

Param's involvement with a low-caste girl upset his father very much. He imagined that he might have a nice time in England like many middle-class Tamil men do, and then come back and marry a high-caste, rich Tamil woman from Colombo with a good dowry.

When he got the letter from his father saying that he no longer considered him as his son, Param shrugged his shoulders as he knew that his father was never going let him make his own choices in life. So Param got on with his life. When he married Mary, his mind was filled with guilt; he couldn't forgive himself for betraying Karthiga. He had never meant to get involved with any other woman except Karthiga, but things had happened which he considered were out of his control.

Now he was in Sri Lanka after so many years, and he had to see Karthiga. He had never considered that he would see her again. He had come to attend his father's funeral and return to London to his family as soon as possible. His plans were thwarted by his sister falling in love with the man who happened to be Karthiga's brother.

It seemed that in this world, whatever we want to avoid comes upon us suddenly. He couldn't do anything else but to go and see Karthiga and talk about Sabesan and Banu.

How would she react, and how would he feel seeing her? Like two strangers meeting and saying hello to each other?

He walked instead of getting onto the bus to Dehiwala. He didn't have to look at the roads. He knew Dehiwala very well. The sun started to go down on the Indian Ocean, but it was still so hot and sweaty. There was a crowd of people going by in a funeral ceremony. He walked like a zombie, his present feelings overwhelmed by the memory of the past.

For a minute, he thought that he just couldn't face meeting Karthiga, that he would find some way of avoiding it. But he had to meet her to sort out his sister's problem. He didn't want to disappoint Banu.

Param was not religious. If he had been to the temple in the past, it was because young men went there to look for girls. It had nothing to do with the thousands of gods who were worshipped by Hindus. But now he prayed not to meet Karthiga. He walked up to her doorstep.

He could tell that the house belonged to a Tamil family. The veranda had a few pictures of Hindu gods and goddesses; there was a *tulsi* plant which was worshipped by Hindu married women for bringing long life to their husbands. There were plenty of roses and marigolds in the front. A little dog was fast asleep under one of the jasmine trees.

He stood there for a minute or two. He couldn't bring himself to press the bell. Ringing the bell became a metaphor for his future. What lay on the other side of this door? He rang the bell hesitantly and waited nervously.

It was Friday. Most Tamils went to the temple on Fridays. Although it was only about five o'clock in the evening, it was still too early to go to a temple for the pooja, yet there was no noise in the house. Maybe an old couple lived here.

He rang the bell again and waited. He could hear faint steps coming towards the door. His pulse started to speed up. He could hear his heart beating. His mouth felt dry, a lump stuck in his throat. His whole body suddenly went cold, and his mind went blank. He wanted to run away. He couldn't stand straight; he leaned on the wall and waited to see who was going to open the door.

He fixed his eyes on the door. It opened very softly, he could see her fingers and then just her face through the door.

Suddenly the whole world went silent and dark. There was nothing he could hear or see.

He fixed his eyes on hers. He could see Karthiga's face suddenly go as white as a corpse. They both stood numbed for a minute or two. He could sense her heart beating faster than his. Her eyes were so big, surprised to see him. He closed his eyes for a second. He didn't think he could bring any words to his lips.

He didn't want to stare at her, so he looked away. Around the house were jasmine and roses in many colours and shapes. He felt that the whole world was cursing him, including the little dog who had just got up and started barking at him. He wished she would shout and scream at him, curse him and hurt him with words.

But she just stood there still as a statue, without a sign of emotion. He wanted to run away, to bury his heart where no one would see. His mind started to boil. His heart was not beating fast anymore.

He wanted to kneel on the doorstep in front of her and cry. He could tell she was not married, yet. She had no *thali* on her neck, no red spot on her forehead.

She was wearing a light blue sari with a red border, just like when he'd first seen her, and a red blouse; they were her favourite colours, and she looked elegant in them. She had a thin gold chain around her neck.

He looked at her again.

'Will you forgive me?' he wanted to cry out loud. But he could not do that.

She was holding the door very tightly. He could read her thoughts from there. She didn't want to cry or scream or even acknowledge him as the man she'd once loved. Why should she?

He felt so small and worthless in front of her. Her image seemed larger than a few minutes ago. If she opened her mouth and told him to get lost or something he wouldn't have been surprised, but...

'I... I...' he started to talk but words wouldn't come out of his throat.

'I... I came to see Sabesan,' he finished the sentence with a trembling tone. He was surprised that his voice was so weak and crackling.

'Sabesan is not home, yet.' Her voice was as clear as a temple bell, not nervous as he thought it would be.

'When will he be home?' he pulled himself together, trying to be strong and sensible.

'I have no idea, he may come home any time or not at all.' She was so business like. She didn't ask him whether he had any message for him, or why he was looking for Sabesan.

'Will you tell him that I would like to see him?' He turned immediately. It hurt him to spend another minute there.

He could hear the door shut, not in the same way it had opened. Now it had meaning, she didn't want to shut the door on him. He felt that behind the door she was just standing there, wondering whether she had just seen a ghost from the past. He could tell that she didn't really believe that it was Param she was talking to. He still couldn't believe that he could talk to her like that, as a stranger. He could still hear what she had said to him just before he went to London.

'I wish I could come with you.' She was crying on his shoulder. It was a beautiful night. They were in their usual place, on the beach.

'I don't want to leave you, either,' he had said very firmly.

'But you see, I have to help my sisters to get married, otherwise, my family won't let me marry you.' he said to her.

'I know, I wish I had lots of money to give to you,' she said sadly. She was not a rich girl. She was the daughter of a schoolteacher who had four other girls and two boys to support.

'I hate the dowry system.' She got up and looked at the stars.

'So do I, but our people are trying even harder to get dowries from the girl's families. It's all to do with education.' To him it was degrading for men to get money from a girl in order to share their life and love together. 'I wish I had the power to change this society,' he had said angrily.

'You wouldn't marry anyone for money?' she suddenly asked him.

'Of course, not, silly, I would never sell myself for money. I'll be back in no time, and I will marry you. It doesn't matter how angry my parents will be with me,' he told her.

He had never imagined a scene like the one he had just experienced, so cold. Everything he had said to her long ago now seemed to play back in his ears loud and clear. His tender words to her back then when he was in love now sounded like a thunderstorm in his head. Falling in love is easy, but getting out of it was not.

Sometimes, he would wake up in the middle of the night thinking that he was sleeping with Karthiga, to find Mary next to him, instead. Many nights he stayed awake thinking that he wouldn't ever get away from the past.

He'd argued with his conscience at times to justify his actions, yet he could never get away from the guilt. He loved Karthiga, and he had really wanted to come back home to her, but getting into the situation with Mary was his own fault, and so he had to accept the consequences.

But after seeing his little daughter born, he was so delighted and so pleased that Mary hadn't had the abortion. He really didn't want to think about anything else except Meera. She changed his feelings about his past. She gave him so much pleasure.

He cursed himself for being a dishonest bastard but tried to forgive himself. After a while, marriage, the child, a mortgage and a good job, his life in England, all kept him away from the past.

Now many years later, he found himself in a mess again. He hadn't even been able to stand in front of her, feeling so small and worthless. He walked into the lane, shying away from the main road. He turned to the beach and walked very sadly.

His feet burned in the soft sand of Dehiwala beach. His mind didn't register anything around him as he walked with his memories. This world he lived in today, he felt, it was full of opportunists and dishonest people like him. You can cheat anybody but not your own conscience, he thought.

She has no *thali*. No *pottu*. She is single.

I am a coward, a very cheap coward, he told himself as he let himself get wet in the waves. I couldn't face reality. People like me use women like Karthiga to feel the satisfaction of manhood. I chased her for months before she even smiled at me properly. I wrote many letters before she replied to one of them. Now what? I have moved away from her life, but she cannot do that. Like most Hindu women, she will put all the blame on her fate and suffer silently.

He walked towards Mount Lavinia. There were many people passing by as there was a big tourist hotel nearby, a standing history of the colonialism. One of the oldest and a residence of the British Governor's s from since 1806. A fabulously beautiful hotel for tourists, but he couldn't look at them. Most of them were probably like him, selfish and cruel people who hurt others, who would love a woman and then just leave her.

'Hello.' Param came back into the real world. He recognised Sabesan with no problem despite the years' passing.

'Hello,' Param said, very officially. When Sabesan was only ten, he would do anything for Param just for a box of chocolates. Now Param didn't know how to address him. He seemed not only equal in height but equal in maturity, too. Param wanted to say, 'I went to see you just now, but I saw someone else whom I never wanted to meet,' but he didn't. He kept the smile on his face to cover his internal turmoil.

'I heard you were home,' Sabesan sounded friendly and casual. As a poet and passionate about politics, according to Sathyan, Param had expected Sabesan to be difficult to deal with.

'Yes, I came back rather suddenly.'

'I am sorry about your father,' Sabesan said very politely.

Param shrugged his shoulders, and said, 'Who can stop people from dying? It was such a sudden illness; anyway, we all have to face the end of our journey sooner or later.' Param suddenly realised that the tone of his voice was different. He stopped himself from saying, You and my sister are partly to blame for my father's sudden death.

'Shall we sit?' Param pointed to the rock near the wave. The sun started to go down. The people on the beach were packing up to go home. The two men walked to the rock and sat there. Param was fiddling with the edge of the rock. Sabesan put his sandals away and let his naked feet touch the waves which were lapping against the base of the rock.

'So, you write poetry, I hear,' Param started.

'Yes, a small-time writer, you might say,' Sabesan smiled modestly.

'What do you write about?' Param asked him casually.

'What do you think I should write about?' Sabesan replied.

'Who am I to tell what you should write?' Param said with an uncomfortable smile.

'Nowadays, people write for lots of reasons. Money, politics, name and fame.' Sabesan laughed loudly.

'I wouldn't know. I am not a writer or a poet.' Param was still trying to keep his voice cool and normal, but he didn't like Sabesan laughing at him.

'There are plenty of things you can write about, but no one can write unless they want to say something and share their experience with others. As one of the oppressed Tamils in this country I write about our struggle,' Sabesan stated fervently.

'You don't have to tell me your politics or the principles behind your writing. I am not interested in politics, nor do I have any intention of getting involved,' Param wanted to say, but he kept his mouth shut.

Sabesan seemed confident as well as handsome. He was tall and slim and had pleasant features. No wonder Banu fell for him.

Sabesan noticed that Param was looking at him carefully, and Param could see this made him shy.

Param looked up at the sky. The sun had nearly gone down to the horizon. There was a slight dimness beginning to cover them. It was a lovely scene, with a dark red sky.

'Banu told me about you,' Param decided to come to the point.

'Oh?' Sabesan did not sound surprised. He turned his face to Param wearing a charming expression.

Param might have said, 'My sister told me that you're a Tamil nationalist and also a bit of a nut,' but he didn't. Param did not go in for emotional outbursts.

'I hope you are not going to give me a lecture on the matter,' Sabesan pushed his wavy hair back and kept his gaze on Param's face.

They stayed silent for a while, then Param said, 'I think you'd better think about our family first, before you tackle the society outside.'

Suddenly Sabesan's expression changed. His face hardened, his eyes fixed on Param's face. 'I see.'

'I don't think you do.'

'Meaning what?' Sabesan's gaze was as sharp as his tongue.

'Well to start with, the difference between you and Banu.'

'Do you mean our caste?'

'Well, not only that...'

Param had not finished when Sabesan interrupted, saying, 'I think we'd better not continue this conversation.'

'Why not?' Param asked Sabesan.

'Now, I know the reason why you betrayed Karthiga. It's your family, isn't it? Your family and your responsibility to keep up your high-caste prejudices, they all came before my poor sister. Is that it?'

Param hated people introducing subjects which he didn't want to discuss. He felt angry with Sabesan for being so offensive.

Param's voice was as sharp as a knife, 'I don't think I have to discuss the past with you. I don't like people poking their noses into my personal matters.

'Oh, I see. If my sister's matter is not my business, how come your sister's matter can be yours?' Sabesan's voice was very firm.

Param felt irritable and uncomfortable and had no wish to continue the conversation. The night started to cover them, and they could no longer see each other's facial expressions properly. He understood Sabesan's anger, yet Param still thought he was behaving badly.

'Hello, Param.'

Param turned back to see who was calling him. There she was.

Liz Baker.

# Chapter 8

Param felt immediately relieved. Partly, he was happy to see Liz, and partly, he wanted to stop the conversation with Sabesan. Liz looked so different. She wore a happy, hippy style, a long batik skirt and a blouse, and she had her hair up in a bundle like a fisherman's wife in Sri Lanka.

'Hello, Liz,' Param got up to greet her. She was with a few other white people.

They looked at Liz and at Param, and one of them said, 'See you back at the hotel, Liz,' and left.

The hot air turned into a cool breeze as the beach darkened, the sky was decorated with millions of twinkling stars and a half moon. The moon was so beautiful and bright, its image reflecting brilliantly on the sea. Her smile was radiant, and she looked gorgeous against the splendid background. She seemed to bring warmth and gentleness to the place. Suddenly the uncomfortable atmosphere had become bright and attractive.

Param introduced Liz to Sabesan, 'She is a journalist, so you two have something in common.'

'Oh, you are a writer too?'

Sabesan shook hands with her reluctantly. Param could tell he was overwhelmed by Liz. She sat next to them on the rock and let her feet play with a wave. She was looking very happy and pleased to see Param.

'What a coincidence running into you here. I thought we might never meet again,' she said.

'This is a small world. How are you coping with the hot weather?'

'I was up in the hills last week, so I was fine, then, but I'll cope.' She smiled.

'Are you here to do some writing?' Sabesan asked her.

'No. I'm just here to see the beauty of Sri Lanka. What do you write about, anyway?' she asked Sabesan.

Sabesan didn't hesitate to answer, 'At the moment in Sri Lanka the burning issue is the Tamil national question and the struggle by Tamils for peace, freedom and justice. I believe writers and artists should reflect the politics of the society they live in.'

'You cannot dictate what artists should or shouldn't do,' Liz said in a defensive tone. 'Artists should have free, flexible minds to create whatever thing is right to create. I don't like uniformity. Art should be free from everything.'

'Don't talk nonsense, there is no such thing. All art reflects the background the artist comes from. There is no art without politics,' Sabesan argued his point strongly.

'Exactly, exactly,' Liz agreed. 'But you see,' she continued, 'I don't believe that artists should be used by the people who are in power nor those who want power. There are many countries at the moment forcing artists to produce propaganda rather than literature for people to enjoy.'

'Art has always been staged to promote the state,' Sabesan countered.

'Not always, but I wouldn't deny that most art has been produced to promote mainly the upper class.'

'What do you write about?' Sabesan asked Liz.

Param got up and walked away from them for a few minutes. He wanted them to understand that he didn't want to participate in their conversation, because he knew that if Sabesan started to talk about Tamil nationalism, Param might say something which would provoke an argument, and he had no intention of arguing in front of Liz. His point of view about the Tamil struggle was very different from

Sabesan's, but he didn't want to engage in arguments with him. 'Arguing doesn't change anything,' he believed.

He stared at the stars and the sea.

He could hear Liz's voice soft and gentle. He felt happy to have met her.

'My writing is mostly about women and oppression. I am not a separatist feminist, but I am a campaigner for fundamental human rights for everyone. I would like to travel and study women in various parts of the world. It is very interesting and sometimes very upsetting to see systems which are supposed to be equal for everybody but always seem to be biased against women.'

'Of course, but people have to fight and struggle for their rights and freedoms. This has to be achieved through struggle.' Sabesan said.

Param turned back when Sabesan had finished talking. 'But the oppression of women is very different from the oppression you are talking about,' Param said to Sabesan.

'No one would deny that Tamils face oppression by the Sri Lankan government. Whereas Tamil women face oppression by their own society.' Param said carefully as he did not want a big argument in the beach at night.

'I am not denying that at all; all I am saying is that I have no intention of writing superficial, fantasy novels or poems. I would rather write realistically about contemporary society and see what we can do to change it.' Sabesan said.

'Change won't come about unless we have real political understanding,' Param replied. 'There's no point in crying about oppression and then go about fighting against it in the wrong way.'

'What is the wrong way, in your view?' Sabesan asked.

'There are lots of political opportunists who are using the situation for their own ends. They are using the youth's passion in order to achieve their own goals, and that is wrong. People have to produce their own leaders and have to unite to fight against the oppressive state. It is no good people declaring themselves as leaders and letting the youths die for their fanaticism.' Param replied in his soft tone so as not to provoke Sabesan.

'People like you can come and say things like that,' Sabesan snapped. 'It's easy for you to make statements because you never have to suffer state terrorism, do you? You can leave the country and escape the government's murder and torture. You don't have the right to make comments on issues which have never affected you.' Sabesan was practically shouting now.

'It's no good personalising it. I am only talking about the general situation. I don't believe in taking a gun against the government unless you have the political strategy to go with it. There's not much difference between a bandit who kills others for money and people who kill others for power,' Param said clearly. He had, after all, allowed himself to be drawn into arguing in front of Liz.

Sabesan got up. He looked upset, but Param couldn't read his face clearly because it was dark. Liz just listened to both their arguments.

'Mr. Param, people should have the honesty to keep their promises. You can't accuse people who are taking arms against a state which is out to destroy a nation. Your brother was never murdered by Sinhalese security forces; your sister was never raped by the Sinhalese army.' Sabesan's words sprang out like fireworks in the silent night.

'What did you say?' Param could hear his voice. It sounded so alien. Then he shouted, 'What did you say?' He could feel his body starting to boil.

Did he say that one of his sisters had been raped by the Sinhalese army?

Now Param understood Sathyan's remarks some days ago. He'd said, 'You cannot understand Sabesan's anger; his family went through hell. Sabesan's brother was murdered by the security forces, and one of his...' Sathyan hadn't finished the sentence.

Sabesan had four sisters, all of them living in Jaffna, except Karthiga. If any of them had been abused by the Sri Lankan army it would be...

'Do you mean Karthiga...?' Param could hardly get his question out.

Sabesan looked at him defiantly and said, 'Yes, my sister Karthiga was destroyed by the racist bastards, the woman who guarded her virtue and virginity, the woman who wouldn't let her boyfriend touch her before marriage, she is the one who was abused by those thugs.'

Param held his head up to the sky. He could hear Sabesan's footsteps moving faintly away from him. He could see his figure far away. There was distant thunder, the noise of the train, waves crashing on the rocks, the long dark night.

Param sat on the sand. He wanted to bury himself in the sand. He'd rather die than digest the thought of Karthiga being raped by a gang of Sinhalese soldiers. Chastity was prized as a virtue in Tamil women. When it came to morals, sex, virginity and virtue, Karthiga was a strong-minded woman. She hadn't let Param go any further than he should have when they were lovers.

'Come on, Karthiga, we are going to get married. What is wrong with making love now?' he was going to ask her once, but he wouldn't as he knew her point of view, giving oneself to another is sacred and there should be a very special connection, not based just on lust.

She knew what he was thinking, and she would shut his lips with hers and say, 'Please don't ask or say anything. Wait, my darling, I wait, you will come back from London, and then we will get married. After that, there won't be any fuss.'

She would have waited for the ceremony, the marriage, the announcement in front of the crowd, the rituals with the priest.

Param had forgotten all about Liz. She sat there without speaking, knowing something had upset Param deeply.

Part of the time, Sabesan had been shouting at Param in Tamil, and she hadn't understood what was going on. But she realised that these two men were upset for some personal reason.

'I wish I... could disappear, now,' Param told Liz.

'What's wrong?' Liz asked him gently.

'Everything is wrong in this country for Tamils at the moment, Liz.'

'I know,' she said.

'I don't think you can understand, Liz.'

'I suppose not.'

'Oh, God. Oh, God. Why is this happening?' He sounded like a child.

'You are very upset, aren't you?' she sounded like mother when he was a child.

She responded like Mary did when he was upset and confused.

'Upset? Oh Liz, how can I explain it to you?'

'I'm ready to listen if you want me to.' She moved next to him, very close, like a mother trying to comfort a child. Her face was so close he could feel her warm breath on him, as when she was on his shoulder in the plane on their way to Moscow.

'Oh no, oh no,' He held his head down and beat the sand with his fist. 'Oh no, I can't bear it.' His voice was trembling. She knew he wanted to cry.

'How many Karthigas have been destroyed in the name of politics? Did they ever harm the government? Why do the innocent have to suffer?'

'Do you want me to go?' she asked him.

She didn't want to leave him, and at the same time she didn't want to force him to tell her why he suddenly got so upset.

He looked at her. He couldn't read her expression, it was so dark. He remembered many nights like this, many years ago with Karthiga on the beach.

Poor Karthiga was not only betrayed by him; she was also abused by the racist army.

'Oh, God, why did she have to suffer so much?' he cried loudly.

Liz stayed silent. She understood that he was upset because of a woman. She leaned close to him and held his hand tenderly.

'Oh…' He buried his face in her shoulder. How could he explain to her about his agony? Would she understand if he told her?

'Liz, I am sorry.'

'Don't be. If you want to cry, that's good, men have this stupid idea that they shouldn't cry.'

'I not only want to cry. I want to destroy the system which oppresses innocents, Liz.'

'It's a cruel society we live in, and sometimes the innocent get hurt, Param.'

'I wish I were strong enough to get my head around it.' He sounded helpless and hurt.

'Why are you so very upset?'

'Because, because the woman I loved has been… oh, no.' He couldn't bring himself to explain anything. Liz waited for him to continue. She did not want to intrude his inner thoughts.

'Liz,' he closed his eyes.

'Yes,' she was ready to listen to him.

'You understand the pain of being in love, don't you?'

'Do you mean have I ever had a lover?'

He didn't answer.

'I don't mix sex and love together,' she continued. 'I thought I was in love many times when I was young, but I don't think that was real love.'

He got up and walked for a bit. Then he lay down on the wet sand and stared at the millions of stars in the sky. The night was cool and silent.

'I wish I were back in London,' he said.

'You don't see stars like this in London,' she said jokingly.

'I don't see lots of things which I don't want to see,' he mumbled.

'Sometimes we have to see, we have to face up to lots of things which we don't want to see or face.'

'You sound like my mother,' he said.

'I'm a woman; we have to deal with life as it comes.'

He sat up and held his head in his hands. Liz felt sorry for him. The image of him in dark near waves some kind pity on him.

'Can I help, Param?' She asked gently to get him out of the wet sand.

'Yes, buy me a drink. There are plenty of places for the tourists to buy drinks,' he mumbled. 'Please join me for a drink?' he asked her.

'Of course,' she got up.

'I want some vodka.' His voice sound so low and strange.

She hadn't seen him touch a drop of vodka in the USSR.

They got up and walked to the Mount Lavania Hotel, where Liz was staying.

They stepped into the bar, and he ordered a Bloody Mary. Param drank it quickly and ordered another.

'Why don't you join me?' he asked her. She said, 'No thanks, I'm fine with my passion fruit juice.'

He was getting drunk. She watched him like a mother watching an upset child. She thought Param didn't want to be himself, he wanted to forget who he was. She watched him drinking heavily. He was not talking a lot, he stood up, staggering slightly, and looked at the bar.

'I think you've had enough,' she said, getting up. 'Can I arrange a taxi to take you home?' she asked him with concern.

'No. I want to go to the beach.'

'It's getting late, Param' she said. She could not stop him.

He walked towards the entrance and stood there. After dark the Colombo beaches are not safe, which Param knew perfectly well. Muggers would appear with knives and demand money, watches and jewellery.

Whether Liz knew this or not, she was worried about his drunken condition, and she followed. He turned back and looked at her. He remembered the hotel in the USSR, where he had nearly asked her to spend the night with him.

She came up to him and held his hand. She didn't want to fall on the rocks around the beach.

There were couples on the beach, kissing and doing other things.

'May I kiss you?' he stumbled. She didn't answer. She knew he was completely out of his mind.

'I am sorry, Liz, I am out of my mind, now,' he said politely.

She did not say anything. She wanted him to return to his normal self; he seemed so disturbed.

'I met my former girlfriend today,' he said, staring at the sky with millions of stars.

She said nothing, listening carefully.

'Did you hear me?' he raised his voice.

'Don't shout, I am sitting right next you, Param.'

'Okay, I want to talk to you, Liz.'

They sat silently on the sandy beach for a while and watched the waves.

'I used to come here with her a very long time ago, before I went to London... Now, I have a wife in London and a child. But I always felt I never had a real friend who would understand me and listen to my story.'

She sat silent and watched him. He could barely hold himself upright; he was falling over with drunkenness.

'I have forgotten lots of people from the past. Well, I thought I had forgotten, but whatever my past is, it turned into the present. I wish I had never come to Ceylon.'

'It seems you came to Ceylon or Sri Lanka now to get drunk.' She was trying to make a joke.

'I came to Sri Lanka to do my duty for my father's last journey and was forced to take part in my sister's future plans. Today, I met a woman I was supposed to marry, and another shock was...' He started to weep.

Liz liked him crying. 'Get it out of your heart, my dearest', she wanted to tell him.

'I feel like crying, too,' she said sadly.

'Why do you need to cry?'

'I'm leaving for New York tomorrow.'

'Why, does your boyfriend want you there?' he said nastily.

'My sister has taken an overdose,' she said quietly.

'Oh, I'm sorry,' he said.

'Thank you. It's her life, if she is trying to finish it, what can I do?'

'Is she okay?'

'I have no idea. She has taken an overdose a few times before, but this time she really wanted to finish her life.'

'God, Liz, I thought I could talk to you about my life and my problems, it seems we all have something.'

'You are drunk, Param, there's no one in the world who has no problems.'

'Well, most people are not asking for problems, are they?'

'You didn't ask for trouble.'

'No, neither did Karthiga.' His voice was cracking.

'Karthiga?' Liz voice expressed her question.

'Do you really want to know who she is to me?'

'If you want me to,' Liz said to him gently.

He sat there, looking at the dark sky. He looked lost and vulnerable to Liz.

'She was my girl, a very long time ago. She is Sabesan's sister. He just told me that the woman I loved, the woman I was going to marry and the woman who always thought of femininity and virginity as the highest virtue for a Hindu woman, was raped by a gang from the Sri Lankan army.'

'I wish I hadn't heard that, I am sorry,' Liz's voice was cracking with emotion, now.

'You don't need to be sorry. There are lots of other people who need to say sorry. Politics is a dirty game, leaders do nothing but create trouble.'

She held his hand.

'It's all to do with politics, Liz. Tamil people never really understand what their leaders are up to. Until the mid-1960s, Tamil leaders were talking about non-violent protests against oppression. But they never reflected most Tamils' aspirations. They had lands and estates in the south and lived in Colombo. Every time there is an election the situation gets worse. Sinhalese political leaders play the race card, sacrificing Tamil issues to get the votes of the Sinhala masses.'

He stopped talking. She had begun to understand why he hated to talk about politics. He was to her a man with certain, values and guidelines which he guarded very carefully. She thought, he wouldn't let himself be manipulated by emotional, racist or religious politics.

'People are always used by politicians,' Liz said quietly.

'Continued oppression made the Tamil people look for alternative structures; opportunist leaders took the chance to promote their personal aims by using Tamil youths. When I was a young man we organised a non-violent protest, but it was destroyed by the army. Most of the Tamil youth became militant from that point. Some of us went to England, but the majority of youths really believed that the armed struggle was the only way to gain freedom for Tamils.'

'Why do you think that is not the answer?' she asked.

'Whatever I see and hear is not a good answer for the Tamil problem, before I went to UK, I was in Colombo, and there was a protest against the upper caste who were not allowing the lower caste to enter the Hindu temples in Jaffna. My friends were involved in the struggle to support the victims.

'But the higher caste who have political, financial influences and with Police support they beat the progressive Tamil students and burned the oppressed people's houses. That time or now, they do not think that the oppressed Tamils are their equals. Now, the Sri Lankan forces are doing whatever they can do to suppress the Tamils in Sri Lanka, regardless of the caste or class of the Tamil community.'

'When people are forced to fight back, they will do it anyway, whether we like it or not,' said Liz. 'If the Tamil people want to wage an armed struggle, are you telling them to stop?' She had not understood the complex ethnic issues in Sri Lanka.

'I am not telling them anything. But it is dangerous to drag a small nation into an armed struggle against a well-equipped and well-funded government.' He was trying to explain to her the reality of the issue.

'I don't want to argue Sri Lankan politics with you, Param, but I don't like to see you upset.'

'I'm upset because of what's happened to Karthiga. Many Tamil women like her have been abused. It's wrong; and I feel I am partly to blame for it. If I had been here and married her these things wouldn't've happened.'

'Don't blame yourself. How can you reverse the past?' she said in a soft tone.

'Can't I? Even now, if Karthiga wanted me to marry her, I would divorce my wife and do it.' His words were blended with so much emotion.

'Param, you are very drunk, you will say different things when you see the daylight.'

'Maybe yes, maybe no. Who knows what else will happen before I leave here, I may be arrested, as my sister's boyfriend is a Tamil revolutionary.'

# Chapter 9

When he woke up the next morning with a splitting headache, it was already nearly midday. His head felt like it had been battered by a rock, and he couldn't open his eyes, either. He didn't know where he was for a minute. His sister's house was noisy with children and some visitors.

'How are you, Uncle?' His niece came in with a cup of coffee.

'I'm okay except for a bit of a headache.'

'Yes, you didn't wake up early this morning. Mother said you weren't well.'

I'm really not well. How can I be healthy and happy after seeing Karthiga and hearing what has happened to her? he thought.

He couldn't remember how he had got home the night before. He remembered talking to Liz on Mount Lavinia beach and telling her about Karthiga and the racial riots. Also he remembered he was telling Liz that he wished he hadn't come to Ceylon. But he couldn't remember anything clearly after that. He felt so embarrassed about it.

Was I walking along? Did I make a scene in the street? Was I singing or talking loudly? He didn't remember anything at all. Did Liz bring me home?

If Liz had come here last night, what would his sister think? What would she think of him 'running around with white women' so soon after the death of his father? Would she think that he was the kind of man who couldn't keep away from women for a month, or something? He felt very uncomfortable with all these thoughts. He lay there for a long time and tried to remember what had happened.

Suddenly, he remembered the conversation with Sabesan last night and imagined Karthiga's face and her tear-filled eyes. His heart began to ache again.

How am I going to face the woman? he thought. Liz had said last night that the emotional outburst was due to the fact that I felt guilty about Karthiga's present situation. How else could I feel? I wish I had never gone to London. If I had stayed here, we would have shared this life together. Oh, God, why have you given her so much to deal with?'

He still needed to talk to Sabesan about Banu. That meant he would have to go to their house again. Yesterday he went to see Karthiga, the woman he betrayed. Now, if he went, his mind would boil to think of what happened to her at the hands of the Sinhalese soldiers. He felt so helpless.

'Are you awake?' His brother-in-law came into the room.

'I think so…'

'The taxi driver said your friend told him that you weren't well. It was clear you'd drunk a bit.'

This was all news to him. Then he began to realise that Liz must have put him in the taxi and told the driver that Param wasn't well.

He thought, Liz, you are very clever, even though you've been in Colombo for only a couple of weeks, you understand the people's mentality. Most Sri Lankans are narrow minded when it comes to the subject of men and women. They would blame a woman for seducing a man, and they would throw all sorts of dirty names at a woman who is seen with a man, Liz must have understood the culture a bit, and knew to stay away from it, and that's why she didn't come in the taxi with him.

Would he ever see her again? She told him that she would be going to New York today to see her sister who had taken an overdose. Some people don't want to live; others who want to live are stopped by others.

He wished she were still here. He could talk to her about Karthiga in detail and even introduce her. He could also have shown her the most extraordinary scenery in the world. He felt so lonely waking up.

'Gowry is coming from Jaffna today. Her fiancé wants to get on with the visa business,' his brother-in-law announced.

Why do they have to rush Gowry's marriage, he wondered, but didn't ask, because there was no point arguing with them. They were not to be blamed. The system was there to make sure traditions were continued.

The legal part of Gowry's marriage had already taken place before their father died in order to expedite the visa application, but the religious ritual would have to be performed in London. They couldn't do it in Sri Lanka because they had to wait until after the thirty-first day of mourning for their father's death. His family said that Param must take responsibility for organising the wedding in London.

He didn't like Gowry's husband Mahadeva at all, but he had no choice.

He got out and went to a travel agency near Fort station to confirm his return ticket to London. Fort was full of tourists from western countries, and he thought about Liz again. Would she be flying to New York, now? Had anyone seen them together last night? It would give the Colombo Tamils some good savoury gossip.

Had anyone seen me going to Karthiga's house? Although the story about him and Karthiga was old, for a few people nothing was too old, nothing would be left out.

They would dig the dirt up and have a dirty gossip for a while, some people never cared who got hurt by the spreading of nasty stories.

If anybody had seen him with Liz on the beach at night, especially Mahadeva's family, or if anyone had seen him visiting his old girlfriend then later holding hands with a white woman on the beach, that would definitely affect Gowry's marriage.

He stayed in bed feeling tired and lonely. He wanted to go home and be with his family in London as soon as possible. He wanted to take Mary to the theatre, he wanted to take Meera to Brighton beach as she loved chasing the waves. He wanted to join with Mary with her gardening duty as she was a girl from a village in Dorset with a huge garden and she spent hours on end in their small garden in Islington.

He thought for all those years in England he had hidden from the memories of the past. He had to come out to face the reality of them in the present, but he couldn't find the strength. Now, he was with his family and friends from his childhood, but felt lonely, alone most of all feeling of lost in a complex of changing outlook on lifestyle and survival.

The next day Sathyan came to see him with his never-fading smile, and Param was cross with him. If Sathyan had come with him, he thought, the situation might have been a little less tense.

They took Param's niece and nephews to the zoo, where they ate ice creams and sweets and watched the animals very happily while the two friends talked.

'Sabesan seems a very stubborn and passionate person,' Param said in English as he did not want his niece and nephew to hear if they said anything about Sri Lankan politics.

'What are you going to do?' Sathyan was a saint. He never showed his feelings.

'I don't know. Banu expects me to help her to marry Sabesan, but he seems a difficult person to deal with. He brings politics into everything, and his point of view is very different from mine, and also, I have no idea how my mother is going to take the news of her beautiful, clever daughter Banu marrying outside our caste.'

'You can't blame people like Sabesan', he continued. 'He is dreaming to change Tamil society which is divided by caste, class, educated snobbery and regional bigotry. Our Tamil leaders were unsuccessful in bringing about a solution to the Tamil problem. These young men think they have been passive and obedient to the Sri Lankan government for too long. They have been discriminated against in education, employment and in all the political structures in the country. We were all born here as Sri Lankans. Why should we have fewer rights than others? There is nothing wrong with fighting for our rights, but the problem is the way people are fighting for it.'

'You're supposed to be a socialist. Why are you supporting nationalists like Sabesan?'

'I am not supporting nationalist fanaticism. It's no different from Sinhala chauvinism. Sinhala fanaticism has brought riots, chaos, destruction and civil disorder. But I think Tamil nationalism will result in more oppression by the Sinhala racists.'

'What is the solution, do you think?' Param questioned Sathyan.

'I think it will take time for people to forget their painful experiences, but there is no alternative but to unite together and fight for freedom for all in Sri Lanka. Up to now the socialist leaders were wrong in their analysis of the Tamil national question. They didn't recognise the

Tamils' struggle, because none of them understood the depth of it. And when the Tamil struggle was led by the Tamil bourgeoisie, the socialists stayed away.'

Sathyan added, smiling, 'As for Sabesan, it's Banu who wants to marry him, not you.'

Param stayed silent for a minute. He was going to ask about the incident in which Karthiga suffered, but instead he thought about himself and Karthiga. After learning about the life she had led for the last twelve years he felt not only guilt but also pity for her. All these years he was too frightened to recognise the truth within himself, but now it was like an open wound. Being in love makes people suffer silently.

He didn't want Banu to suffer in the name of love. When human love meets with opposing forces such as money or power or the caste system, it sometimes dies away. Maybe it dies away from sight. But invisibly, someone in love never forgets. They never really forget.

Param felt an obstruction in his heart. He couldn't tell anybody about his agony, and he couldn't tolerate the emotion of seeing Karthiga. He had to go and talk to Sabesan about his own sister Banu.

That Friday he took himself to Dehiwala to see them again. He phoned home and talked to Mary and Meera. Somehow, it wasn't joyful talking to them.

'Darling, I miss you,' Mary said to him.

He didn't say I miss you, too. He said, 'I want to come home.' He wanted to escape from the reality of Sri Lanka.

He wanted to be in the arms of Mary to feel secure, loved and wanted. He felt guilty for not telling Mary about his past with Karthiga, but Mary was the one who did not want their past to mix with their future.

He never explained to Karthiga why he suddenly stopped writing to her. How could he tell Karthiga, who was waiting for him to come home, that he was going to be a father in London?

He walked to Karthiga's house in Dehiwala from his house in Wellawatta via the beach. He wanted to talk to Karthiga, to ask her to forgive him for what he had done to her. He would do anything to make her happy, that's what he thought. That's what he told Liz, as well.

People were gathering on the beach to enjoy their evening at sunset. He just walked like a zombie, not able to acknowledge the beauty or the people around him.

He entered the lane where Karthiga lived. His stomach started to feel funny, and his mouth went dry. He rang the bell and waited patiently. Like the previous week the little dog who was sleeping under the jasmine tree barked for a minute. He waited patiently.

She opened the door. Like last week she was calm and stable. Wearing a pink sari and a red blouse. She'd let her hair down to dry after her bath, before she went to temple.

'Come in.' Her voice was so gentle and calm.

He walked in. He remembered going into her house many years ago with a very happy feeling.

There was a noise from next door, children playing. There was no sign of Sabesan at all. She went in and sat on the settee in front of him, as he let his eyes wander around the room. There were Lenin, Mao and other socialist figures on the wall alongside Hindu gods and goddesses.

'I'll get you a drink.'

It was like two old friends were just having evening drinks together, as if this were an everyday event, and he was confused by her behaviour. Her calmness frightened him. He didn't know what to expect next.

She came in with a tray full of snacks and soft drinks and left the tray on the table.

'Karthiga,' he said.

They held each other's gaze for a few seconds.

Her face was so sad, and her lips were trembling with emotion. Her eyes filled with tears.

'Please don't cry,' he begged her.

She looked like a small girl who had hurt herself.

'I am sorry,' he said.

'Please don't say sorry.' She wiped her tears with her sari.

He wanted to cry with her. He felt he would have been more satisfied if she had shouted at him or cursed him.

But she very calmly said, 'Don't say sorry.'

She poured a soft drink and gave it to him. He took the drink from her.

'Sabesan is not at home.'

'I noticed that.'

'I wanted to talk to you, Param,' she said, whilst watching his expression very carefully. 'But please don't think I am going to talk about us or about me,' she made it clear. He prepared to listen.

'I have to talk to you about your sister Banu and Sabesan.'

He poured himself some more of the soft drink.

'He is mad about his politics. I don't know how much he is in love with your sister.' she said.

'She seems very much in love with him,' Param said while looking into her eyes.

'Oh yes, but then falling in love is the simplest thing in the world, but how many stick to their guns until the end?' She seemed to be talking to herself.

Is she indirectly questioning me? he wondered.

His fingers played with the tablecloth nervously as she continued. Whatever he was thinking to say to her stuck in his throat with guilt.

'I think he is working with one of the militant groups campaigning for our struggle. There are many being murdered by the security forces. Hundreds of Tamil boys have disappeared. You don't know what has happened to my family.' She found it hard to stop the tears.

Yes, I know what happened to your family and to you, he wanted to scream. But he held back so as not to upset her.

She looked so vulnerable and needing help.

He wanted to kiss her, comfort her, but he found it hard to bring himself to talk to her truthfully.

'One of my brothers was murdered by the security forces. My mother has become mentally ill. My father is very ill. As you know I have three sisters who are not married. Do you think you could help Sabesan to get out of the country for a while?' she asked him, while trying not to cry.

'I will, Karthiga. Please don't cry, I will do anything I can to help you.'

'Don't say that. I didn't ask you to do anything for me. You can do this thing, but it will not be for me. It will be for five Tamil women, your sister, me and my three young sisters. We have no one else in the family to look after us except Sabesan. If he gets into trouble, we have no one to look after us, Param.'

Now, he understood why she wanted to see him. She wanted Param to help Sabesan to go to London. He was not going to tell her that he had already made a plan to help his sister Banu to leave Sri Lanka and get Sabesan to follow her to London.

'Your brother seems very stubborn,' he said. He wanted to say, if your brother loves my sister, he must do something to save their future.

'So do lots of Tamil young people,' she said sharply; her voice was firmer than usual.

Taking arms against the rapist Sri Lankan military is unavoidable as their atrocities are horrendous. Is that what she was trying to say?

He recognised some aggression in her tone, but he didn't want to analyse it. 'Yes, it's no good being stubborn about matters which are beyond our control,' he said.

'Being stubborn?' She hadn't sat down, yet. She was standing in front of him asking questions, like a teacher.

'I don't believe that the Tamil militants will achieve anything by armed struggle without constructive political ideologies, and taking innocent young minds and making them fanatical about their politics would fail sooner or later.' Param pointed out his views on Tamil militancy.

'It's easy for you to say things like that. You come to Sri Lanka now and then from the land of affluence and the life of luxury. How can you understand what we are going through?'

Her words went through his heart like an arrow going through leaves. 'Please don't tell me I don't understand other people's suffering. I may not share it, but that doesn't mean that I don't acknowledge it and…'

They both stayed silent for a while. He wanted her to talk to him. He didn't care what she said, but he wanted her to talk to him. He might never have a chance to talk to her again. They might never see each other after he returned to London. This might be the only chance they would have to see each other alone, so he wanted her to talk, to talk about anything. He wanted to remember this meeting forever. It didn't matter if, at the end of the conversation, she told him she never wanted to see him again, that she would only see him for her brother's sake.

'I will do anything I can to help your family,' he said in a determined tone.

'But please, don't do it for me. I wouldn't be happy with that. If my brother fell in love with someone else's sister, I would ask the same of him. I don't want you to think I…' She started to cry.

He had never let her cry when they were lovers. He had always done or said something to stop her crying.

'Please.' He got up.

She suddenly dried her eyes and said, 'Sorry if I upset you by crying, but there are lots of things which have happened to me, most of them I can't tell anyone about.'

'Karthiga, you can tell me anything. I will never be a stranger to you.'

'Better to be strangers, and please don't bring up the past.' She spoke quickly and got up. 'I will bring some food.' She went into the kitchen.

Had she cooked for me? he wondered. She came back with some vegetarian food. He had been a vegetarian before going away to London, and they often used to go to Wellawatte Luxury Hotel for a vegetarian meal.

She left the food in front of him, the vegetable dishes reminding him of the past. He went to the kitchen to wash his hands as she served the meal.

This was all like a dream. All those years ago he had dreamt about this scene. Their getting married, having a family, eating food she cooked and her watching him. It was happening now, but they could no longer feel the same things for each other.

'You said it would be better to be strangers, do you mean that, Karthiga?'

'What's the point of having dreams when one knows the reality of life?'

'I suppose so.' He started to eat. She was there watching him. 'Won't you join me?'

'I'll eat later.'

'You are still a traditional Tamil woman, aren't you?'

'Is there any alternative?'

'But you are strong, Karthiga.'

'I'm not, really.'

'I… I… I'm sorry for…'

'Don't keep on saying the same word, Param. The world is not going to turn back twelve years; we must accept what's in front of us and get on with our lives.'

'Will you ever forgive me, Karthiga?' The words came with the pain of the last twelve years.

'There is nothing to forgive, Param. You made the decision to live in London, and that's all there is to it. But I wouldn't deny that I had many dreams, and in the dreams, I always wanted to cook for you, care for you,' she said weeping.

'I know… I am sorry… I never meant to leave you.'

'Please don't keep saying you're sorry. I believe it's my fate. I have to suffer like this. I will never blame you. When I knew that…' She couldn't continue to talk. She buried her head on the table and sobbed.

He got up and came behind her, holding her head on his chest. 'Karthiga, I am not going to ask you to forgive me. I do not deserve that. I would be happier if you really cursed me and called me a dirty bastard.'

She turned and put her finger on his lips as she used to when they were in love, and said, 'I will never say that… I love you. Still, I pray for your happiness. If you are happy, that's all that I want.' She held his hand very tight.

'My God, I never thought we would meet like this. Karthiga… I must tell you a few things about…'

'I told you, I don't want to know anything… Not now.'

'But I must tell you, when I went to England, I was lonely, I was unhappy. And London gives people the freedom to do anything they want... I was... well...'

How could he explain about Mary, who was a true friend when he was alone with no close family and only a few Sri Lankan friends in London?

How much would Karthiga understand, when Mary took him to her parents and introduced to him as her 'close friend'? How could he tell Karthiga that Mary saved him when he had was attacked by the racists? How could he tell her that he never stopped talking about going home to Sri Lanka, but when they went to a Christmas party their young minds and the exciting environment brought them together?

That closeness brought changes. Mary said, 'I am pregnant, I am a strong woman and I love children, but I never wanted a bastard child. If you acknowledge our baby and go home, I will tell the little one that its father had to go away but he loves you. But if you do not want that, if you don't want to have anything to do with it, I will abort the baby.'

He was with Karthiga now like a child lost in a jungle of horror and quietness.

She looked at him, he was like a small boy wanting to blame anything and everything for the past except his own actions.

'London is a world with its own philosophy, own culture, own manipulations. I am a weak man. I got into this other world, let myself go. Freedom can mean anything, including letting your memory fade away. Then I got involved with a woman who was very much in love with me... time went faster than I ever imagined. When I knew that I was going to be a father I didn't know what to do...' He stopped talking, and his voice went quiet.

'I'm not asking you for an explanation, Param. Why do you have to dig up the past?'

'Maybe, maybe because I wanted to tell you myself or clear up a few things.'

She turned her face away from him as she knew he wanted to talk regardless of whether or not she wanted to hear.

He continued. 'Mary was prepared to go for an abortion. I knew I was in love with two women, and also, I knew that somehow or someday one of them might call me a bastard, but what could I do? I thought I shouldn't give a damn about what others said about me, and I should do what my conscience said was right. I was deeply upset about losing you; at the same time I couldn't let a little human be aborted in the name of our relationship. You may never understand what I went through. In the end I went ahead and got married, it was cruel of me from your point of view. But I never told Mary about you. If I were honest, I should have explained to both of you and put a stop to all my mental agony ages ago. But in my mind, I knew what I had done to both of you. I was not a good man to either of you.'

She looked at him and said, 'That's an easy escape, feeling sorry for yourself and thinking that's enough to make it alright.'

'I'm not looking for justice from you… I'm only trying to say…'

'Why can't we just forget about it and help the young ones to live together. My brother could be captured by the army at any time. Then I will lose a brother, and your sister will lose her loved one. Can't we do something to stop it?' She sounded desperate. She was begging him to protect her family by helping her brother get away from the situation in Sri Lanka. She had only one brother, with responsibility for four women in her family.

'Yes, I must, I do not want my sister to go through what I went through in falling in love with someone from another caste. I will help my sister and Sabesan to be together,' he promised her.

She was always thinking about other people. The poor woman never learned to live for herself; that was the way she and other Hindu women were brought up. According to Hindu beliefs a woman should carry the burden of keeping the family name and prosperity.

'Please stop worrying about others for a change, Karthiga,' he said.

'Look, Param, I have no life left, I have no illusions about my future, nor do I have a dream of having a husband and children. I have learned to live with the reality of being a Tamil woman in this country, and I will be lucky and happy if I can help others.'

'That's an easy escape, too… don't you understand that by getting involved with other's problems it gives you temporary pleasure, but when you sit down one day and think about yourself you will realise…'

Her sharp look stopped him from continuing.

'Well… what I'm trying to say is that…'

'There is nothing much to say about me, Param.'

He looked at her with pity in his eyes, but he also wanted to make her understand that he was desperately trying to inspire her to change her life.

'Better not get involved with more than we can tolerate.' Karthiga said this in a clear tone, as she sensed some childish comment or more outbursts were coming from Param. He wanted to finish his meal and leave as quickly as possible before anyone saw him here. He didn't want her to suffer from the gossip of the Tamil community in Colombo.

She started to clear the table; maybe that was a signal for him to leave. He looked at her for a minute while she worked. He thought, if I really want her to be happy and to have a secure life, I must think of some other way to achieve it.

They could hear someone coming.

'Well, should I say goodbye, now?' he asked, his tone was soft and his expression sad. They both knew they might not meet again.

He went for a long walk in Victoria Park in Colombo to think things over. The park had changed, too, like everything in Sri Lanka. Victoria Park was in front of the old British old Town Hall and next to the Museum. It once had rare Sri Lankan flowers and plants, but now it seemed to be decorated with mostly western plants and shrubs.

The gardeners seemed to be concentrating on their care very delicately. Karthiga loved colourful surroundings, even her simple sari and blouse had a certain style and meaning. Today she had worn a plain colour sari and a matching blouse, and she had looked splendid in it.

'Oh, Karthiga, what can I do to make you happy? I wonder if I'm overreacting because of guilt. Am I trying to make her happy or myself? How much do I have to reorganise my life to please Karthiga and feel good about it? What will happen to my relationship with Mary when I go home with all this pain in my heart? All these years I thought I had forgotten my past, but now it seems well in control of me. How can I deal with it rationally and realistically?'

I wish Liz were here in Colombo so I could talk to her, he thought, but in the next minute he said to himself, what on earth am I thinking, that Liz would have some interest in my life? After all I've only known her a short time, so why am I thinking that she should have an obligation to listen to my woes? This is my life, and I'm going to deal with it in my own way, he told himself like a little boy determined to change for the better.

There were a few couples in the park who seemed to be in love, kissing and whispering as if they were the only people in the world. Would those young men behave like me one day, leaving their loved one and marrying someone else?

How would their girlfriend react? Put the blame on God and get on with her life? He realised that Karthiga was stronger than he had expected her to be.

So am I going to be… well, was there any other choice? he told himself.

# Chapter 10

Param's family was discussing many matters resulting from their father's will and trying to sort out Gowry's and Banu's future. He played his role as head of the family. He told them that he had a plan to take Banu to London.

The whole family was shocked. 'Why?' they chorused together, in a high pitch. They were confused and looked at him with a surprise in their expression.

He said, 'Gowry will be in London soon, why shouldn't Banu come and study something there? She'll be able to do whatever she wants, remember she wanted to be a lawyer like Uncle Indran when she was only eight years of age?' Mother was in complete confusion as she never considered that Param might take Banu to England.

'She… She…' his mother was trying to tell or ask something. His sisters were looking at him trying to tell him not to upset Amma.

Oh, in that case I have to leave Banu and her future in at their mercy? he thought. Why should I let them bully Banu? She's done nothing wrong by falling in love with Sabesan. If she can manage to live with his artistic temperament that's up to her.

The family was trying to tell him that their mother needed Banu's help.

He said, 'Geetha would be happy to have Amma in Colombo. I will send money if Geetha needs any help.'

None of them said anything after that.

Banu came to Colombo from Jaffna a few days later. He took her to get a passport, visa and all the other necessary things.

'I should ask Sabesan,' she declared.

'About what?' Param was cross that Banu was already under Sabesan's control. He added, 'Oh yes, be like a Satya Savitri in Hindu mythology, who will do anything her man tells her to do.'

She didn't like his remarks about being a passive woman. She said, 'My dear brother, look here. If you think you are going to stop me loving Sabesan by taking me to London, you can forget it. I am not going to do what you did to Karthiga...'

'Stop being a child, Banu, I'm taking you to London because I know Sabesan loves you enough to follow you. Otherwise, you think that our family will ever allow you to marry him? They'd rather kill you, Banu, for falling in love with him. And think about the political situation here, your lover will be a meal for the Sinhalese racist hunters in no time.'

'How do you know that he will follow me?'

'If he loves you enough, he will listen to me and come and study something for a while until the situation gets better in Sri Lanka.'

She could see her brother's mood had changed a lot over the past few weeks. She didn't know that he was doing it all for Karthiga, all the while making a show of taking responsibility for his family.

For Param, he could not give a minute of thought to what others might think about him. It made him feel relaxed and peaceful to think at least he was doing something to please Karthiga.

For a few days he ran to and fro like a madman in Colombo booking the tickets and everything for Banu. Everything for Gowry who was going to come to London with Mahadeva, was done by Mahadeva's family.

He wished that he could do something for Karthiga to change her life, too. Would she ever get married, or did she believe that she was doomed to suffer forever?

He couldn't imagine her growing old with no one to love and care for her. She was such a wonderful person; she could offer so much towards creating a family with a man. If I could manage to talk her into getting married, would she listen to me? he
wondered.

One afternoon he was rushing around in Colombo Fort when he met Sabesan and Karthiga. Param was very happy to see them both together and brought up the subject immediately.

'You know, I am trying to take Banu to London.'

'Well, she is your sister.' Sabesan's tone was sarcastic.

'Do you care about her future? Do you?' Param questioned Sabesan. He felt relaxed talking to Sabesan in front of Karthiga, but Sabesan looked at him angrily.

'I care about all the Tamil women being raped and murdered by the Sri Lankan armed forces.'

Param did not want to argue with him.

Param walked with them to the bus stop. There were people everywhere. Sinhalese, Tamils, Muslims. This is how it happens. Now and then a riot breaks out, and some people in the crowd get murdered. All because of religion, politics and language. What barbarism!

'Param, I may be a young Tamil militant who has different political views from your own, but I am at least honest enough to stay here and face the problems and fight for peace, freedom and justice for my Tamil nation. Who are you to ask me whether I care for the woman I love? Did you care for the woman you loved?' Sabesan asked him.

Param wanted to hit him in the middle of very crowded Fort station. But he controlled himself and said, 'I understand your hatred towards me, so I am not going to debate with you. But I hate you for bringing the subject up in front of the person who is involved. I thought you were more decent than that.'

Karthiga tried to shush them, not wanting them to argue in the middle of Colombo. 'Sabesan, will you leave my past with me? Don't ride on my back,' she said to her brother angrily.

'I am sorry,' Sabesan said to his sister after a while.

They walked along the crowded Colombo fort area and went to have coffee as a group of good friends.

The atmosphere eased, Param enquired, 'Where are you two going?'

'Karthiga wanted to go to the cinema. I don't like these stupid Tamil films. But what else can a Tamil woman do? There are only a few places they can go. One is the temple. The other is the cinema where they preach at you to be a woman who does everything for a man.' Sabesan's words were like a fireball.

Param laughed at Sabesan's commentary on Tamil films. 'I don't like women who do everything for a man, either,' he said, indirectly addressing Karthiga. He wished she could marry someone and be happy, rather than living in the memories of the past.

She looked at him with a questioning expression.

'Can I come with you?' Param asked Sabesan.

'If you can tolerate the emotional stuff.' Sabesan laughed. They went to the cinema, where, as they expected, it was all about a woman who was doing everything for her husband.

Param and Sabesan exchanged their remarks on traditional Tamil films, whilst Karthiga suffered during the heroine's cries.

'If I had the power, I would shoot all the writers, creators, poets and film producers who portray women as creatures with no individualism except to give themselves to the men whom they marry,' Sabesan declared.

'I thought you wrote for people who wanted to think and change society. Is it good to just shoot all the people we don't like?' Param hinted at Tamil militants who murdered moderate thinkers who didn't like their militant politics.

Sabesan said, as they came out of the cinema, 'It's inevitable in order to destroy the enemy within.'

Karthiga looked at them, her eyes saying, please don't argue.

'I have to meet someone somewhere. You will be okay, won't you?' Sabesan asked Karthiga and left.

Karthiga and Param waited for the bus to take them home. She was looking around very nervously. She didn't want to be seen with Param.

'If you want me to go, I will go,' he said. She did not say anything.

The bus came, and they both got on as they used to when they were students at the university in Colombo. She sat near the window and put her head out, staying silent. After a few minutes he noticed that she was crying, and he felt very uncomfortable about it.

The Tamil film was very like their story. Two lovers couldn't get married because of their caste differences. The man's family wanted him to marry a woman from his own caste, and the woman, who was low caste and very much in love with him, asked him to marry the woman whom his family had chosen. The lover refused, and in the end, the low-caste woman killed herself in order to let her lover please his family and live happily ever after with his wealth and prosperity.

'Please don't upset yourself because of the silly film,' Param ventured.

'I am not crying because of the silly film,' Karthiga replied.

'What is it, then?' he questioned.

'Please be careful. There may be some Tamils on the bus,' she whispered in his ear.

'Oh yes, yes. There are Tamils all around the world. Shall we go and bury our heads in the sand?' He was cross to see her behaving like a woman who was constantly thinking and worrying about others.

'It's all right for you to ignore our traditions. But we have to live here, whether we like it or not, these are our people, and there are rules and regulations to obey,' she told him firmly.

'Shall we go somewhere?'

'Why?'

'I want to talk to you.'

'About Sabesan?'

'No. About us,' he said firmly.

'There is nothing to say about us.'

'There are plenty of things we have to discuss.'

He was determined to get her off the bus, and she knew that if she didn't get off, he might drag her off. When the bus stopped at the next stop, he got out and she followed him reluctantly.

'You just said you don't like women who do everything to please men,' she accused him.

'I don't want you to please me. I want you to think for yourself. Our Tamil traditions are preventing our women from thinking for themselves,' he snapped at her. They walked towards Kollupitya beach. It was a cool evening, and people were heading to the beach for fun and relaxation.

There were a few hostels around the beach for university students.

He suddenly remembered waiting on the beach for her to come from the girls' hostel when they were young. He knew that she would be remembering the same thing.

'I don't like this place,' she mumbled.

'I know,' he said sadly. Who wanted to suffer from the memories?

The beach was crowded as usual. Most of them were young couples, because of the nearby university hostels. He could feel her anger, and also her confusion as she hesitantly followed him.

Why should I go with him? she thought. She shouldn't worry all the time about others, he had said. Maybe he was right. Was he any help to her when she suffered at the hands of the Sinhalese rapists? Could anyone stop her brother being murdered by the Sri Lankan armed forces? How many people cared about her mother being mentally ill? How many would really come to help her sisters who were getting old without a dowry to buy husbands? She hesitated for a while. He would leave for England soon, and she may never see him again. Well, it wasn't as if she was walking with a strange man. Karthiga decided that at least once in her lifetime she should talk honestly to the man who was in love with her.

They sat on the rock. A wave came and crashed at the foot of the rock, and the evening breeze eased her mind. She knew that he was watching her very carefully.

'What are you thinking?' she asked him.

On the way here from London he hadn't expected to see Karthiga like this. He'd even thought that she may be married with children. It was strange to imagine her with another man.

'What do you want to talk about?' she asked him while looking at her watch.

'What did Sabesan say about Banu going to London?' Param asked her.

'Nothing much. He loves her very much. If she is happy going to London, that's enough for him, he said.'

'So, he is going to stay in Sri Lanka and become a freedom fighter.'

'I don't know what he will do, but I will be very happy if you can get him to London, too.'

'I will do my best. Banu said that he would come, but not yet. She said give him a few months to think things over. I will be going to London soon, then I'll do what I can do.'

A train passed by going south. Some people waved to them with friendly gestures. Even though they were strangers they waved to the people they saw.

'Will you bring your family when you come next time?' she asked him. He looked straight into her eyes but didn't answer.

'What is the matter? Are you happy with your family?'

He didn't answer her question.

'Sorry if I asked you a personal question,' she apologised.

'It's not that you asked a personal question. Until I came here, I was very happy with my family, but to tell you the truth, I don't know whether I am going to be happy after seeing you like this.'

'Oh God, don't say that. I don't want you to feel guilty about the past.'

'Karthiga, I don't know how to stop feeling guilty about letting you down, and I wish I could do something to make you happy.'

'In that case you know my answer. If you are happy, that's all I want.'

He leaned closer to her and held her very close to him. First, she started to look around to see whether anybody they knew were around. But the darkness covered the beach completely, and streetlights were starting to flicker. He saw the reflection of the flickering lights in her eyes.

She cried silently.

'Please, Karthiga, don't cry.'

'Some people hardly every cry. Women like me have nothing much to smile about, and so we cry instead.'

'There's no need to feel self-pity. Making or breaking is up to us sometimes.'

'Really?' she smiled at him sarcastically.

'I don't mean that your experiences in the past are of your own making, but isn't it time to think about making your life better?'

'Making life better,' she repeated his words very sadly.

'I wish you would get married,' he said the words very carefully.

'What?'

She nearly jumped out at him but he held her tight and told her, 'Look, Karthiga, I love you. Really, I do. But I can't put the clock back. I could divorce my wife if you wanted me to, but I don't think I will do that, or that you want me to do that. I love my wife Mary and my daughter Meera more than my life, but I am not going to be at peace after seeing you in this way. Please, please, think of doing something to change your life for the future.'

'Oh, stop talking nonsense.'

'I'm sorry to see you like this, Karthiga.'

'Please don't pity me.'

'Well… if you don't want others to pity you, do something different and useful.'

'Such as getting married?' She was angry, her voice was harsh.

'Yes,' he said firmly.

'Do you think women like me... like me... who are left by one man and used by many men have any future of... Oh, God, don't you understand? I can't... I cannot be a good wife to anyone,' she yelled.

'Why ever not?' he demanded an answer.

'Param... let down by one man and raped by many...'

'Don't say it, Karthiga. Don't say it.' He cried with her. He didn't want to think about it; he didn't want to hear it from her. 'My darling, you have the purest love to offer any man you will marry. You have the most beautiful mind I have ever known. Please, please get married and be happy. I would feel better if you were contented. That's what I always wanted.'

They stayed in each other's arms for a long time.

# Chapter 11

He had to rush to get things ready to go back to London. He hadn't been able get a passport ready in time for Banu to go with him, and Gowry was in the same position. They all thought it would be better for both girls to go together.

It was the thirty-first day after the death of Param's father, and the rituals had been carried out according to religious tradition.

While he was in Jaffna there was another political killing by a Tamil Tiger militant. They killed a CID officer who was a government informer betraying Tamil militants. As soon as the shooting happened, Jaffna town had filled with Sinhalese armed forces. They went into shops beating people, beating them without regard to whether they were man, woman or child.

Param happened to be in a taxi going home, and the driver hurried to get out of the way of the army. Somewhere in the town the killing went on, and somewhere in the city the people were suffering.

There were roadblocks. Param's taxi was stopped and searched for the militant Tamil Tigers. Param couldn't understand the Sinhalese language, and the soldiers didn't understand Param's English or Tamil.

'It's a pity we don't have a common language,' Param said to them, but they were shouting and screaming in Sinhala about the Tigers.

If I were a Tiger, why would I be arguing with you? he wanted to say to them.

One came up to him and slapped his face, and Param's blood boiled. Jaffna was his own hometown, where his family for generations had been born and brought up, where he had played as a child. Now, he was being attacked because he didn't speak the language of foreigners.

Suddenly he remembered something Sabesan had said. 'Everybody has fundamental human rights. No one has the right to take that away just because someone belongs to a minority nation which does not have the political, military or financial influence over the majority government.'

At home, Banu was in turmoil, worried about Sabesan. She suspected that he might have been involved in the shooting; he had come to Jaffna only a few days ago from Colombo. She hadn't seen him or spoken to him since the incident, and she wanted Param to go to his parents' house and see whether he was home or not.

He was very reluctant to go and see Karthiga's family in Jaffna, knowing that her father knew about his and Karthiga's relationship. Karthiga's father, maths master Mr. Sivam, was a very progressive man. In the course of his tuition he would also talk to Param about changing society, abolishing the caste system and fighting for equal rights for women in Hindu society.

The old man told him that he was in India during the late thirties and was involved in the Indian freedom struggle. One day, he said, India would have to go through a long struggle to eradicate corruption before anyone could think of fighting for socialism. He said he couldn't see how a country that was so strongly influenced by religion could be in the hands of a bunch of people who had nothing better to do than exploit millions of hard-working Indian people. Whether nationalist politics, or progressive politics, he used to say that there was no freedom for individuals unless the individual belonged to a nation which was free from all oppression by other forces and from within.

In those days he had also listened to his friend Sathyan, who was already involved in radical politics in Jaffna. Sathyan was seriously involved in the late sixties in a campaign for the right of temple entry for low-caste people in Jaffna. The middle- and upper-class Tamil Hindus vigorously resisted requests from low-caste people to enter the Temple to pray. Param had been busy writing love letters to Karthiga whilst Sathyan was writing slogans for equal rights for the oppressed caste in Jaffna and Sathyan was beaten up by upper-class Tamils many times. Karthiga's father was one of the old people who joined the progressive forces against the Tamil feudalists who wanted to maintain caste prejudice.

As Param thought about how reluctant he was to meet Karthiga's father, all those memories flashed back into his mind. But he agreed to visit, as Banu was in tears with worry. He had to wait until the Sinhalese police and soldiers had gone from the main streets.

When he went to Mr. Sivam's, it almost looked like a deserted house. Not much was happening around the veranda, where there always used to be students waiting for tuition. When he reached the house, he could hear *Veena* music. The beautiful *Kalyani Raga* mingled in the air. He opened the gate. He stopped and thought back to when he first saw Karthiga chasing a little goat.

He went up to the veranda.

'Who is that?' The old man came out. He was very and frail now, a sad looking figure.

'Me... me, Paramanathan.'

'Param... Ooh... Param from London?' The old man came up to Param and tried to look at him closely.

'Oh yes, you look different, now. A big man, a very big man, indeed,' the old man said, but he didn't ask Param to come in.

'I am looking for Sabesan,' Param didn't want to put him in the position of having to invite him in.

'I think he went to Colombo in the morning. Mind you, he never tells me anything nowadays.'

Param didn't know whether this was the truth or not. Perhaps his father knew about Sabesan's involvement with militant Tamils, and perhaps he knew whether he was involved with the killing of the CID man today.

'Is there any message for him?' he asked Param.

'I'd rather speak to him, if I can,' Param said very politely. In the meantime, he could see someone coming onto the veranda.

'Sabesan has gone to Colombo.'

Param recognised the woman standing on the veranda. She was one of Sabesan's sisters, her name was Kogila, and she was a very good *Veena* player. She looked very straightforward and easy-going, and Param felt that she was telling the truth.

'He will be with Karthiga,' the father said.

'I know, I met them,' Param said.

Mr. Sivam fixed his eyes on Param. Is he indirectly asking, why don't you leave my daughter alone? Param thought.

'Would you like a cup of tea?' said the old man. Still he didn't ask Param to take a seat.

'No, thanks. I have to go to Colombo tomorrow, and I have so much to do, thanks, anyway,' he said, and tried to leave.

'Will you ever come back and live here?' the old man came out with him to the gate.

Param turned back and looked at him.

'No, there is no point in coming back here. There is no dignity, no identity for Tamils in this country, now. Who knows how long it would take for our lives to get back to normal?'

The old man had lost one of his sons, his wife was in a mental hospital, one daughter had been gang raped; his only living son was involved with militant activity. What was the old man's future going to be?

He did not ask Param, 'why are you looking for my son?'

Did he know that his son was love with Param's sister Banu?

Even if he knew the story, he doesn't look like he'd have the strength to stop Sabesan.

In that minute of seeing Karthiga's family, Param made up his mind to take Sabesan to London, at least for the time being. It was not only for Karthiga's sake, but also for everyone in Sabesan's family. On the way home he wanted to sit somewhere in the lane and forget about his life in London.

He belonged to this Tamil society in Sri Lanka, but now, that society had no political or economic future. The younger generation was facing random arrest, torture and in some cases killing by the Sinhalese security forces.

What would have happened to Param if he had come back and married Karthiga? His family wouldn't have forgiven him for marrying a low-caste woman to start with; then he might have become involved in Tamil politics. His life would have been a mess.

Was his life stable now? He sat on the wall under the tamarind tree near the main road listening to the army vehicles passing by. It was a very dark night. Not much darker than the life of Tamils in Jaffna, he thought.

What would his mother say, when she realised her beautiful, clever daughter who wanted to be lawyer and be highly respected in Jaffna society was going to marry a low-caste boy? Would she shout at Param as her husband did to him? Or would she say that she never wanted to see Param again for helping her to marry the man she loves?

If Sabesan takes arms and dies for the Tamil cause, he would be praised as a *maaveeran,* martyr, a freedom fighter who gave his life for his people. But if he marries a high-caste girl, he and Banu both may be killed by the high-caste Tamils to preserve their dignity. What hypocrites the Tamils are. He was asking many questions to himself.

When he reached home, he could see Banu's figure standing near the gate.

'Is he okay?'

He felt the nervousness in her voice. He could tell she had been crying.

Oh, God, my darling sister, so deeply in love with revolutionary Sabesan, he thought.

'Hey, I thought you were stronger than anyone else in the house. I don't want to see you cry,' he said, trying to comfort his sister. She knew that Sabesan was okay, but she still cried.

'Anna, you are not taking me to London to take me away from Sabesan, are you?' she asked him hesitantly.

'Don't be silly, I want you to marry and live happily with Sabesan. That's why I am taking you to London. In a few months' time we will send for him, too. The situation in Sri Lanka is not good for any young Tamil man, now.'

'Thank you, my darling brother, but sometimes I feel that what happened to you and Karthiga may happen to us. Our family and friends will never allow me to marry Sabesan. I cannot live without him. If he dies at the hands of the Sinhalese animals I will... ' She didn't finish the sentence.

He came and put her hands on her mouth and hugged her closely, saying, 'Banu, my sweet sister, I am sorry I did not come to Jaffna for so many years, but I love you all, and I know how much you love him. I will do anything to help you two get together. I won't let you suffer like…' He thought about Karthiga, but he didn't mention her name.

They went inside, where their mother was busy packing things for him to take to London.

'You bring my granddaughter to see us,' his mother told him.

'I will.' He noticed again that none of them talked mentioned Mary; it was as if she never existed. Well, that didn't matter, now. As soon as he got to England he would forget about their remarks about Mary. Whether they liked it or not, that was his life, and he was going to stay with it.

He got up early in the morning and went out for a long walk to Jaffna town. It was still nearly empty, bare of morning traders.

In Jaffna, the bus station had few buses and few passengers. Will I ever come back here and stand at the bus stop again? he asked himself. He went to the bookshop and bought a few rare Tamil books and felt so happy. He used to read a lot of Tamil novels. He was proud reader of Daniel, Benedict Balan, Ganesalingam, Jeeva and other progressive writers when he was teenager and Jaffna. Some of the Sri Lankan Tamil writers had changed the Tamil literary arena in the 1960s. They introduced Dalit literature into mainstream literature. He cursed himself for being so ignorant about contemporary Tamil culture. No wonder, Jaffna still has modern thinkers like Sathiyan, he told himself proudly.

This time he took Sathyan along to go and see Karthiga. He wanted to reintroduce Karthiga to Sathyan. They had known each other a long time ago, but Sathyan was now working upcountry, and had not had the chance to meet Karthiga socially. Sathyan had no idea about Param and

Karthiga's affair twelve years ago, as it hadn't blossomed until they were at Colombo University and Sathyan was at Peradeniya University on the hill side.

Param had no intention of telling him about their past relationship, but he repeatedly asked Sathyan to help Karthiga, because Sabesan might go to London soon, and then Karthiga would be alone in Colombo.

Sathyan said he wouldn't mind going to see Karthiga now and then, but he didn't like Param's idea that women had to be looked after, and on the way to Karthiga's place they argued about Tamil women's position in society.

They talked about women who were involved in militant activity with Tamil youths, while at the same time playing the role of tea-makers and typists, rather than getting involved in any discussion or debate. 'Women are never going to achieve anything unless they want to achieve something,' Sathyan said.

'When the struggle is taken up by the middle class, you only see their interests,' he continued. 'Did you ever see any middle-class men expecting their wives or daughters to become revolutionaries? Revolution will never come unless the masses are ready for it. What you see now is some middle-class boys who couldn't go to university or get jobs in Colombo who have taken the position of political opposition, but I don't think that's enough to make them carry the struggle forward, or to make it belong to the Tamil community as a whole. When the time comes all the people will participate, men, women, peasants and the bourgeoisie.'

Sathyan's lecture was nearly finished when they reached Karthiga's house. She wasn't expecting anyone else except Param. He could tell that she was not that pleased to see Sathyan, but still she welcomed them and asked them to have something to eat.

She cooked some special food for him, and while they were eating Sabesan came home. Param casually mentioned that his sisters were going to London, soon.

Sabesan said, 'You can afford to buy a husband for your sister, what can I do with the little money I earn?'

Sathyan said, 'You could speak against offering a dowry, rather than talking about buying husbands.'

The conversation went on mostly about the increasing amount of dowries in the Tamil community.

Sabesan said that because of the increasing number of Tamil boys leaving for other countries due to police and army brutality, getting a good bridegroom was a serious business now, and the price of a groom from abroad was increasing, too. 'A man from London is worth up to two hundred thousand rupees, and if he has a British passport, the price could be much more.'

Param hated this kind of conversation.

Sathyan said to Sabesan that if his organisation ever came to power, he should tell them to shoot any man who asked for a dowry.

Karthiga busied herself cooking and didn't participate in any of this conversation.

Param ate the meal very happily. Would she ever cook for him again, he wondered.

When he left, Param said to Karthiga, out of earshot of Sabesan, 'It's your responsibility to send Sabesan to London.'

He washed his hands whilst Karthiga said, 'My sisters need to get married, and unless Sabesan has a good job and some money, that is not possible.'

'Karthiga, I really believe Sabesan will come to London because I know he loves Banu enough to follow her, but will you stop worrying about the others?'

They stared at each other for a minute, and he wanted to embrace her, kiss her and say goodbye, but he couldn't.

Everyone came to the airport to see him off, Sabesan, Sathyan, Banu and the rest of his family. Everyone came except 'her'. Param's family seemed to have no idea about Banu and Sabesan as an item, as Sabesan came with Sathyan who was known to the family as a friend of Param since they were at primary school in Colombo.

As the flight took off, and Colombo disappeared behind the clouds, he wondered, would she be thinking about me?

He sat back in his seat and tried to visualise her, but all he could see were Karthiga's tearful eyes. He was going home, but his mind was full of Karthiga, not of Mary. He was completely unaware of the changes that were to come about in his life.

# Chapter 12

'You have changed.' Mary kissed him tenderly as soon as he came through the immigration doors. Param had lost weight, and the hot weather had made him browner than when he left London six weeks ago.

'Daddy.' Meera jumped on him like a monkey. 'I am sorry that Grandpa died. How was the summer vacation? Was it very hot, there? How is Grandma'? Meera had lots of questions for her father.

'You've lost weight,' Mary held his hand whilst they walked to the car. He just smiled at her and kissed his daughter. Suddenly, he realised how much he had missed them.

'So, how were things back home?' Mary got into the car and started driving.

There was a big pause from him. Where can I start? he thought.

He started to tell her about his father's funeral and Gowry's wedding arrangements. Then about Banu's love affair and how he was involved in it all. He had written to her about all those things.

'When is Banu going to come?' Mary asked.

'Soon, I hope,' he said. He was happy that Mary was understanding his predicaments.

'So, you have gained the title of 'man of the house', have you?' she asked him jokingly.

'Well, Mother felt a bit guilty about a few things, such as not consulting me about Gowry's marriage arrangements. Now, she has asked me to organise a nice wedding for Gowry in London, but if she knew what I am doing for Banu with a low-caste boy, she would wish that I'd never come back to Sri Lanka.'

'I don't want you to take on too much. You already look worn out. Imagine having two sisters in London and taking responsibility for their future. Be careful, won't you?' Mary advised her husband lovingly.

It was a Saturday when he arrived, and Islington was bustling with shoppers. This was the world he had forgotten for six weeks. He felt so tired and just wanted to go to sleep. But Meera was excited to see her father after six weeks and asking so many questions about Sri Lanka, while Mary was cooking.

But he felt so tired and wanted to go and rest, so he went upstairs and lay on his bed, looking at the ceiling and letting his mind wander.

He couldn't think about anything else but Karthiga and her sad face. What can I do to make her happy? If you take me back, I will divorce my wife and come to you, he was going to tell her. Would I do that? Did those words just spill out because I was upset at seeing her sad face?

He could hear Meera in the garden. Mary came upstairs and lay near him. He didn't move, he stayed still and silent.

'You look tired. Have a little sleep.' She touched his face fondly. She was expecting him to say how much he had missed her. Instead of that he stayed silent. He didn't go to sleep.

After lunch he phoned a few friends and enquired about getting admission for Sabesan. He phoned Mahadeva and talked about Gowry. Mary watched him making call after call to people in Tamil.

He has to help his family. What can I say? she told herself. She let him make the phone calls and went downstairs.

For the next few days Param was busy trying to get things ready for his sisters' arrival.

Mary said she was applying for a full-time teaching post, which she had mentioned a long time ago as Meera would start secondary school in September. Param would have liked to have another child, but Mary didn't want any more children. He didn't say very much when she told him that she was job-hunting.

Meera was excited about her aunts coming from Sri Lanka and asked him about who was coming to live with her.

Param wrote Karthiga many letters about Sabesan. Karthiga's letters brought various news from Sri Lanka. The situation for Tamils was getting worse by the day.

There were meetings in London by some Tamil organisations; but Param had never participated in any Tamil politics in London. Partly, he was not a political person, and there were other things he didn't like about the hypocrisy of middle-class Tamils in London, self-made men who were trying to gain a name and fame through Tamil politics.

He hated fanaticism. Most of the London Tamils were middle class, and the majority came to London not because they had faced oppression in Sri Lanka but because they wanted a better life. Most of these Tamils were high caste.

Param believed that exiled Tamils shouldn't propagate division, whether between Tamils or Sri Lankans as a whole. As Sathyan put it, 'What do they know about ordinary Tamils who are suffering on the tea estates upcountry and in the Batticaloa paddy fields? Why should innocents have to suffer for middle-class aspirations?'

Having just been to Sri Lanka he suddenly began to take an interest in London's Tamil society. But still, he didn't believe that the way the Tamils were going about gaining freedom was the right way. As the people who are in the forefront of subjects are not from the majority of Tamil people in Sri Lanka, but a very elite of the Tamil community who wanted to keep their high-caste status and were highly influential in controlling Tamil social systems.

He thought a lot about Sabesan and his militant politics. He admired Sabesan's courage and determination to fight for freedom for all the people. People like Sabesan, were they really for the Tamil people and their aspirations?

Mary silently watched her husband's changing attitudes. Learning to live with a man from a foreign country hadn't been easy for her, but over the years they had both adjusted and learnt to live happily together. Now, she was seeing a different person. Param seemed more concerned about what was happening in Sri Lanka than in their own home.

That spring, nearly every day, it rained. The car needed a check-up, and the house needed to be redecorated. Mary mentioned all those things to Param, and although he said, 'Yes, I know, we will do these things,' he wasn't taking enough interest to make them happen.

Mary was beginning to feel restless about her husband's attitudes. She didn't mind that he was taking so much responsibility for his family, but did he really need to spend most of his time making telephone calls and writing letters?

She was a very tolerant person and would never start an argument unless she had good reason to. She loved Param very much. But that didn't mean that she could just ignore his changing moods. She knew that his father had opposed their marriage, and she wondered whether his family had had a good talk with him for marrying a white woman.

'What's the matter?' she asked him one night when they were in bed.

'What's the matter with what?' he asked without looking at her.

'You seem miles away,' she kept her voice down.

'Do I?' he asked her back casually.

'You're doing too much.'

'Yes, I know.'

'You have a family here to think about, too, you know.'

He turned to her, wide awake, now. 'I don't think I am ignoring the duty to my family.'

'Mending cars and doing the shopping. Is that all family life's about?' she
asked.

He didn't answer. What is life? he wondered. Is it a couple living together? Buying a house, paying the mortgage, mending the car together?

She wanted to tell him that their way of life was changing so rapidly, and she did not like it very much.

He knew that for the last few weeks he had not been close to Mary. The Param who had felt so secure and loved in her arms seemed to be somewhere else, now.

The Easter holidays came and went, and their usual visit to her family in the country did not happen. They had never been apart before he went to Sri Lanka. There was a curtain of silence drawn between them. Neither of them knew that a bigger silence was to come.

The streets of London seemed bright and busy, and people were quick to welcome the summer. Param booked a hall for Gowry's wedding. She and Banu were to arrive in a few days. Mary helped Param prepare the invitation list and other details. She helped her husband in his tasks, but it all seemed tiring and alien to her. Too much to handle in a short period.

Param went to the airport to meet his sisters with Mahadeva, but Banu didn't seem very happy to be in London. On the way home they talked about the increasing police brutality in Jaffna, and Param wondered about Sabesan's family, but he waited until they got home so he could talk to Banu alone.

Meera was happy to meet her new aunties, and Mary welcomed the in-laws. However, she had never had to live with others in her life; now suddenly there was lots of activity and lots of people in the house.

Mahadeva came over any time he liked, which made Mary irritable. 'Why can't he phone before he comes over?' she asked her husband.

'It is just our custom that relatives don't phone each other before going to visit.'

'It's not our custom, here,' she pointed out.

But Param, too, didn't like Mahadeva's attitude of taking Mary's hospitality for granted.

Param mentioned it to his sisters on the way to the shops. Gowry remained silent as usual, and Banu said, 'Mary is a very nice person. We shouldn't upset her.'

Mahadeva was already making remarks about getting a higher dowry, saying, 'Your brother is doing well, your family could afford to offer more.' This made Param quite angry.

'Why don't you refuse to marry a man who demands a dowry?' he asked his sister.

'My dear brother, I don't think any woman wants to buy a husband for money, but the dowry system is so strong, and it's traditional; it's not possible to simply refuse,' Banu told him. 'We can't change the system. It's up to men to change it. They are the ones who are selling themselves for money.'

'What will you do if our brother arranges a marriage for you offering a high dowry?'

Gowry asked Banu.

'I don't think my marriage will get to that stage.'

'Why not?'

Gowry's question made Param laugh. 'Banu has already selected her man,' he said.

'What?' Gowry screamed. Normally, Gowry didn't open her mouth much or talk much about others, but hearing about Banu's secret life made her jump.

'What is the matter?' Param asked his sister.

'How can she do that?' Gowry exclaimed.

'So, finding a man who is a bit progressive and modern is a problem in Jaffna?'

Param challenged her.

'Do you have someone progressive and modern?' Gowry asked Banu, but Banu didn't answer.

'Who is he?' Gowry kept demanding, 'Who is he?' until Param said, 'Sabesan, the militant poet.'

'You mean?'

'That's right. Karthiga's brother.'

'Oh, God. He is… he is…' Gowry didn't finish.

'According to you all he is low caste. So what?' said Banu.

'Banu, don't talk nonsense. It can't happen.'

'Why not?'

'Mother wouldn't like it.'

'Mother is not going to marry Sabesan. I am.' Banu was very sharp.

Gowry couldn't say further, she could only mumble something about family respect and what would happen to Banu if she married Sabesan.

Mahadeva invited his friends and relatives to the wedding. The hall was filled with food and people, but on

Gowry's side there were not many. Param thought back to his own wedding to Mary.

After his own family's objections, Mary's family, too. Mary's father hadn't liked his daughter marrying a 'coloured' man to start with, but in the end, they had come to the reception. The couple went to Paris for their honeymoon, and while Mary suffered with morning sickness, Param secretly suffered from the guilt of abandoning his promise to Karthiga by getting into a life with Mary.

He thought about organising a grand wedding like this one for Banu and Sabesan, but he knew that it wouldn't happen. Sabesan was not a person who would like a grand wedding, and Param himself didn't like religious ceremonies and the Hindu priest saying something in an alien language.

He looked over at Banu, who looked very beautiful in her red silk sari. What was she thinking? Was she worried about getting Sabesan to London?

Param left the wedding with Mary.

'Are you pleased?' Mary asked him on the way home.

'I don't like men who use women for their own personal gain,' he said.

Then he talked about Sabesan and why he liked him. Mary said that Param was worrying too much about other people and that he should have been understanding about his family, too. Param said he was fed up with her remarks about him taking care of his family, accusing her of being 'selfish', and they argued.

As any couple they'd argued many times in the past. It was never anything like this, now.

Mary could see that Param was no longer her husband alone, now he was a brother of two sisters in London. He had his duties towards them. For Mary, this was new and worrying, and Param had very little time for her. He had changed a lot. She had no idea why he was so distant from her since he came back. They used to enjoy their sex very much. Now, Mary felt that his mind was somewhere else. Was it only to do with his sisters, or something else? Mary couldn't work it out.

By the time they reached home Mary was furious. As Param parked the car Mary went indoors and went through the mail. She was holding a postcard and asked him, 'Who is this Liz?' Mary's face look like a volcano. Exploding the words as a raging fire.

'I told you, we were on the plane together going to Sri Lanka.'

'I don't get holiday postcards from my fellow travellers,' she said sarcastically.

'Don't start an argument. I'm tired of arguing.'

'Did you see her in Sri Lanka?'

'Yes. I bumped into her on the beach, and we went for a drink.'

'Oh, yes?' Mary's voice was very high.

'What is the matter, now?' He sat on the chair.

'Sri Lanka, moonlight, soft breezes, changing scenery. Was she sexy and romantic, so you had a fucking summer holiday there, didn't you?' she demanded bitchily.

'I don't want to answer your stupid question,' he said, going upstairs.

At first, he thought Mary's attitude was unreasonable; but she was obviously restless about something. I should be taking more notice of what she says, he thought. Once he had sorted out Banu and Sabesan's problems, then he would relax with his family.

'Mary, are you angry with me?' he asked her softly when she came to bed.

She didn't answer.

'Do you suspect me of being unfaithful to you with Liz?'

She changed into her night dress and got into bed.

'Mary, do you think women like Liz have no one else to chase except your husband who is in his mid-thirties, has a stupid face and getting grey hair?' he laughed.

She turned to him, and he could see her eyes full of tears. She came to him and put her arm around him and said, 'You are only thirty-six, a kind person, a handsome, sexy man. I know you never slept with anyone but me, darling, you can please any women brilliantly, and I love you, Param.'

'That doesn't mean that you have to be so silly.' He kissed her.

'You wouldn't...'

'No, I wouldn't.' He comforted his wife whilst she kissed him passionately, and they made love, for the first time since his return.

His mind was wandering to thoughts about Karthiga, and he said to himself, Param, you are a real bastard. You've messed up two women's lives, already. Don't get involved with Liz, as well.

He couldn't lie to himself about the feelings he had had for Liz in the Russian hotel. He had nearly told Liz: If I were not married, I would ask you to share the room with me.

He thought about Karthiga's sad face and Liz's happy face in Tbilisi, whilst making love to Mary. Then he felt sick and tired and stopped half-way through.

'What's the matter?' asked Mary, still with her eyes closed and waiting for him to continue.

'Nothing, I am just tired,' he turned his back on her. She got up and sat near him. He could feel her eyes on his back.

'Are you asleep?' she touched him softly. He didn't answer. 'Param, I am not happy with our relationship, now.'

'Why?' He tried very hard to keep his voice down. 'Do you mean we are not making love as we used to?'

'Don't be silly... I am talking about something else.'

'Like what?' he really shouted at her.

'Don't shout at me,' she snapped. 'Param, your mind is miles away. You said you have to do lots for your family. I understand that, but I think your mind is on something else.'

He closed his eyes. He knew that she was right.

'Will you tell me?'

'There is nothing to tell.'

'Liz is coming to London. Her postcard asks you if you can meet her.' Mary stood up and left the room angrily.

He knew that Mary was suspicious of his mood and behaviour, and she had good reason, too. But he didn't want her to put the blame on Liz. He knew that now that he was home, he would have to change his attitude and pay more attention to making Mary happy; otherwise, something would go very wrong.

That night, Banu came in late from the wedding, with Mahadevan's relations. They were in the kitchen making tea and talking loudly. He went down to tell them to be quiet.

Mary was sleeping in the spare room. What were his relations going to think about his life? Marrying an English woman was one thing. Having separate beds was another matter.

After they had gone home, Mary told Banu that she didn't appreciate people coming round any time they liked without asking her.

Param tried to explain that going around enjoying the wedding party is very natural in the Sri Lankan community.

Because of the wedding, people thought it was okay to drop in on their relations.

Mary replied, 'You are not in Sri Lanka, now.'

Banu had got up early and taken Meera to school, and the morning started with a great silence in the house. Param could feel the tension in the air. He came down to the dining room and found Mary busy in the garden digging something.

'What are you doing?' he said, trying to be pleasant. She didn't answer. He buttoned his shirt, went back inside and sat at the table. Mary was still digging.

He got up to go out, and he saw the postcard from Liz in the fireplace. He picked it up and read it. It simply said that she wished that she had spent more time in Sri Lanka. She hoped that Param was alright now, after his experience there. And she said 'See you soon. I will be in England at the end of the summer.'

He left the card where he found it. He turned and saw Mary watching him, reading the letter.

'Are you still angry with me?' He tried again to be pleasant.

She said, 'Why should I be? If you want to be a playboy, that's your problem.'

He retorted angrily, 'Mary, it's a pity. We seem to have lived together for over twelve years without knowing about each other.'

'I think so, too,' she left the garden fork outside the door and walked in.

'What makes you think I have something to do with Liz?'

'Because you have changed since you went to Sri Lanka.'

'And you think that's because of Liz?'

She didn't answer for a long time. Then she said, 'It may be.'

'I hate to think that I've loved and lived with a strange woman who did not understand me for all these years.'

He left the house in a state of anger.

Getting college admission for Sabesan wasn't easy. Most of the colleges either had no vacancies at all, or else they didn't seem to have any interest in giving the places to foreign students.

Mary didn't like the idea of Sabesan coming to stay with them, saying that Param had taken enough responsibility, already. He said that he had to help his sister Banu to marry the man she loved.

Param helped Banu to get a job in an Indian supermarket, where she had to work very long hours for very little money. Param said, 'Banu, you have to learn to live in London, you have to go out to earn as well as learn English, one day you can go to college, too.'

Sabesan's letter to Banu explained the situation in Jaffna. There were more arrests of Tamil youths and more killings of Tamils by security forces. There was always tension in Colombo, and Tamils were expecting big riots because the racist politicians there were continuing their hate campaign against the Tamils.

Banu was upset every time she received a letter from home; she was worried about Sabesan and the complexity of the situation. She was scared that she may never see him alive again.

To Param, Karthiga's letters from Colombo and Sathyan's letters from upcountry mostly told the story about the situation. Former Sri Lankan Prime Minister Mrs. Bandaranaike's civil rights reforms had been revoked by the present President Jayawardene's regime because of the corruption during her time as Prime Minister.

Param phoned his sister in Colombo occasionally to get general information, but people in London seemed to know more about events in Jaffna than people in Sri Lanka, as the government often censored the news.

There was a general strike in Colombo. Many thousands of workers were dismissed by the United National Party government for taking part in the strike.

Sathyan described the situation angrily, 'Nowadays, there are no civil rights for anyone in Sri Lanka. There is increasing state brutality against not only Tamils, but also trade unionists, civil rights campaigners and human rights organisers, which is making the situation worse. When you look at the leaders of the people, not many trade union leaders or political party leaders come from the working class. Most of them belong to the middle or upper class. So, when struggle arises, the leaders don't want to take the socialist path; they don't want to give up the privileges bestowed upon them by the existing political system.'

Param wrote to him saying socialism in Sri Lanka was based on theories imported from Cambridge and Oxford, not on the experience of people in third world countries. It was time, he wrote, that third world socialists realised it, and started to think about real change in politics by understanding the poor people in Sri Lanka.

Sabesan wrote to Param and said Sathyan had come to visit Karthiga whenever he could, but Sabesan didn't like 'armchair socialists' like Sathyan who still believed that total revolution for Sri Lanka was the only option to sort out Tamil problems.

Param enjoyed the letters from Karthiga. She not only wrote about general things; she also wrote about herself trying to keep happy by going to meetings and talking to other Tamil women in Colombo. 'Thank you for introducing me to Sathyan. He is trying to turn me into a new woman; he is a really kind man.'

Mary was increasingly unhappy with her husband's involvement with his family. She wanted to get Sabesan's and Banu's problems sorted out as soon as possible. Then Param would relax and be happy like the old times, she thought. She was trying to forget about Liz's postcard. She and Param knew there was tension between them, but they were trying to work out how to be happy as a couple.

When Param got admission for Sabesan, he thought about Karthiga's happy face. He said to himself, Karthiga, at least I could make you happy by helping your brother. I know it's not enough to make up for the unhappiness I caused you.

Param finished work late after doing overtime at the office. He was a chemical engineer, working for an oil company. There was a conference soon on world oil markets, and his firm was presenting a report at it.

He got up and went to the window. He could see the river Thames and the many boats going by. He thought about Liz, suddenly, in Georgia, where she was so happy running onto the oldest bridge in the world. Where would she be, now? Her slender figure and her charming smile came into his thoughts.

I wish she were in London, now, he thought. But then he thought he shouldn't be thinking like that, as Mary had been so upset already about Liz' postcard.

The car was in the garage for repairs, so he had to take a Victoria Line train home to Highbury and Islington. It was a cold autumn evening. He hadn't walked much in the past as he'd always had the car. It was a cold autumn evening, but it wasn't just the cold wind, there was also some drizzle. He walked fast to get into the station with his face down, unable to see other people. Victoria station was full of people from the continent and other places via European coach services. He was a stranger, too.

His mind wandered resting on many irrelevant thoughts; he'd been so restless since returning from Sir Lanka.

What can I do to cheer Mary up? he wondered. He wanted to be close to her as he had once been, but now he seemed too far away. Will I ever again be happy with her? He simply had no answer for these questions at all.

I may have to think carefully about how to change my life to make it happier, he thought. Then as he approached the underground station, someone called him. 'Hello.'

There she was.

Liz Baker.

She looked very pale and thin. Having been thinking about her only a few minutes earlier, then seeing her out of the blue like this, his eyes sparked with joy.

'Hello, Liz,' he said excitedly.

She looked happy to see him, too.

He had so much to say to her. 'Are you in a hurry to get somewhere?' he asked her, hiding his overriding emotion underneath a big smile.

'Not at all. I'm just on my way home.'

'Will you join me for a drink?'

He didn't know how to start a conversation. He wanted to talk to her about Sabesan, Karthiga and all the things she knew about.

'You seem very happy,' she said.

'Do I? Well, I am not drunk like the last time you saw me in Colombo.'

'Don't worry, it's better to get things off your chest, now and then, if you have to get drunk to do it, well, do it. I wanted to stay in Colombo and help you, but I had to leave for New York.'

He admired her frankness and was glad of her friendship.

'So, how was America?' He walked her towards the bar near the station. 'Your sister?'

'My sister is still unhappy, but she survived. As for America, there was nothing wrong with America, but the politicians are so high and mighty. They think they are the masters of the universe and have the right to control everything, every country on the earth, it's a pity that one country has taken the role of ruling the world, and other helpless countries let them get away with it.'

'You seem angry with Americans.'

'I'm not angry with ordinary people in America at all, how can I get angry with poor people who have no proper home to live in, no proper health care and no job to go to?'

'That's what this new profit-making society is all about, Liz, the minority holding wealth will always keep the majority of the poor in that condition in order to maintain their control.' He said the words like Sathiyan would say them.

'It's so unfair. At times I feel like destroying the whole universe.'

'Not now, Liz, because I am starving,' he said jokingly.

She laughed softly. 'It's so nice to see you, Param.'

'Let's celebrate this happy meeting, Liz.'

They both went into the bar. He looked at the time on the bar clock; he hadn't told Mary that he was going to be late home. He wanted to phone her, but she might ask why he would be late, and he'd have to tell her the truth. Mary was already suspicious of his friendship with Liz, and he didn't want to start an argument the minute he got home.

Besides, he needed a friend to talk to, just now. Mary was in a miserable mood, nowadays. He was glad to have run into Liz, and he didn't want to spoil it by telling Mary about it.

'How's your family? I'd like to meet them.'

He smiled at her but said nothing. Meeting Mary? He wondered how it would work.

'If you want me to,' she said reluctantly when she saw his uncomfortable smile.

'Of course, you must meet Mary. She is very interested in world peace, feminism and all those things you are interested in.'

Partly he was telling the truth, partly he wasn't. He knew Mary's point of view on world peace, but he couldn't be honest about her feelings concerning his relationship with Liz. Mary already suspected something more than friendship was happening between them, and she had reason to be suspicious of his changing attitudes. Mary couldn't understand that what had changed Param had nothing to do with Liz. Neither could he have explained to Mary about his relationship with Karthiga, not now. This he should have explained before they got married. It was too late now to bring up the past.

'What are you doing at the moment?' He bit into his chicken as he asked her.

'Journalism, freelance. I am planning to do a book on women, marriage and relationships.'

He stopped eating for a minute. Was she reading his mind and his worries about Mary?

'Oh, yes?' he said, trying to laugh.

'Well, my sister's life has made me think a lot about those issues.' She sounded sad. 'I don't know why women have to feel so guilty and upset if their husband looks for another woman,' Liz continued.

He felt terribly uncomfortable hearing her talk about this subject.

'My sister took an overdose because her husband had an affair with another woman.'

'Naturally, she felt unwanted, I suppose,' he chose his words carefully.

'That's why I get cross with women. Why do they have to feel that? If a man goes out looking for more than he already has, let him go. After all, people talk about open relationships a lot, nowadays. But the relationships between men and women are becoming much more complicated than they used to be.' She talked like a woman of seventy years.

'Relationships between people are always complicated, but when people have to think about other things besides the marriage, they simply get too involved with other things and expect too much from each other,' he said pensively.

'You may be right. My sister was never involved with anything or anyone else except him and their two children. When she found out that he had been having an affair for the last ten years, she couldn't take it. But taking an overdose of pills wouldn't sort out anything, would it? She couldn't simply forget that he had been cheating on her and their marriage.'

Param wished that Liz had never brought the subject up at all. Am I cheating on Mary by not telling her that I am out with Liz, by not telling her about Karthiga? he wondered for a minute.

He wanted to change the subject, so he said, 'Sabesan is coming to London.'

'Sabesan?' She was trying to remember him. Param reminded her about the incident on the beach in Colombo.

'Oh yes, the man who shouted at you about Tamil politics. Well, why would he leave the liberation struggle to someone else and come to imperialistic Britain?' she said teasingly.

'Well... He doesn't want to come. I am trying to get him here for lots of reasons.'

'I see, the people who can afford to get away from the state terrorism are leaving the country.' She seemed to know more about Sri Lanka than before. 'If I were in Sri Lanka, I would like to leave, too. Who wants to die at the hands of the armed forces? Anyway, politics is a dirty game. I'd rather not talk about it. How about your... I'm sorry, what is her name?' Liz asked Param.

'Karthiga. She is okay. Well, what else can I say? I wish she would get married and... ' he said.

'Why? Do you feel guilty seeing her single?'

Liz was a woman who valued honesty, he said to himself. She came straight to the point.

'Not really.' He knew that she knew that he was lying.

'I don't like men feeling sorry for women,' she said. 'After all, there wouldn't be any problems if men stopped being greedy, selfish power-mongers.'

'I don't want to argue about men and women and their power games.' He stopped the conversation.

They laughed and joked about food, clothes, books, all sorts of things, and he enjoyed the evening very much. People like Liz are not only pleasant themselves, they create pleasure wherever they go, thought Param on his way home.

# Chapter 13

He got home very late, and Banu was reading a book in the sitting room. There was no sign of Mary.

'Where is Mary? Is she in bed?'

'No, she has gone out.'

'Out?' he looked at the time. It was nearly twelve o'clock.

'Yes, she said she was going to see a play with some friends.'

'Oh.' He felt that Mary should have told him, but couldn't Mary have asked the same question? Did he tell her that he was going to be late? He started to go upstairs but saw Banu's face was restless and unhappy.

'What is the matter?'

'He, Sabesan has sent a telegram.'

Banu gave him the telegram. Sabesan would be taking a plane to London the following day. Param forgot all about Mary as he visualised Karthiga's happy face as she put her brother on the plane.

'I will take time off from work tomorrow. I'll have to find a place for you two, now,' he teased his sister.

She turned her face with embarrassment.

'I hope no one in our family notices what's going on.' He smiled at his sister.

'Well, they're all going to know sooner or later,' she said with a beautiful smile.

'Then you will be Mrs. So-and-So; who cares what others think?' He really felt happy and jolly. He was laughing and joking with his sister when Mary came home. He wanted to tell Mary about Sabesan and also to tell her that he was sorry about the last few months. As Liz would put it, why should people have to lie and hide their feelings from each other? If they love each other, they should be open.

Mary came in without taking any notice of him at all. She changed her clothes, got into bed and was trying to cover herself with the bedclothes.

He felt insulted, but he tried his best to be nice to her. 'Mary,' he called. He wanted to talk things over, but she ignored him. 'Why do we have to behave like strangers?'

He put his arm around her and turned her towards him. They looked at each other for a minute or two without speaking.

He felt so sad to see Mary in that mood. She looked a bit pale and thin. He hadn't even looked at her properly for the last few months. All he had been worried about was making Karthiga happy by helping Sabesan come to England.

He had nearly forgotten all about his wife's needs and love.

Mary started to cry. He kissed her eyes and said, 'Sorry, I have been so busy, I know. I have been a bit out of touch with you, recently.'

She freed herself from his arm, lay back and continued to weep.

'Please, don't cry.'

'I am not crying because of you,' she snapped at him.

'Can we discuss a few things?' he said. Liz had said that most couples never wanted to discuss anything until it was too late. He didn't want that to happen to them.

She turned the light off and turned her back on him.

'I'm sorry,' His words reached her in the darkness.

He could feel butterflies in his stomach. He thought about Liz's sister who wanted to finish her life when she discovered that her husband was involved with another woman. I may not be physically involved with Karthiga, but whatever I'm doing do now is because of her. Maybe it's just because of my guilty conscience, but…

He didn't want to continue those thoughts. He couldn't bring himself to think of losing Mary's love.

He thought about Meera. She was no longer a child. She was going to become aware of the unhappiness between her parents. He loved his daughter more than anything in the world. He wouldn't do anything to upset Meera. He even got married to Mary because of Meera. If for no other reason, he wanted to continue the marriage for her sake.

'Mary, please talk to me.'

'I don't like being treated like an alien… You are treating me like a stranger.

Your life around you, your… well, you're living for somebody or for something, I cannot explain, but that's what I feel,' she said without raising her voice, but he knew that she was right.

'I have not been myself since I went to Sri Lanka.'

'I know, and I don't believe it's only because of your sisters.' She was right, again.

'Well, there are a few things I must tell you.' He began to feel that he needed to talk about Karthiga.

But she said, 'I don't think I want to listen to you.' Her voice was as sharp as her looks toward him.

How could he explain to her about his past, which he himself had forgotten for many years, and which now all seemed to be back in the present, and he had no choice but to play his part in. How could she understand the agony he was going through? People may cheat themselves by pretending they don't want to remember the past, but they often still feel the nagging pain in their hearts.

'You married me because of Meera, didn't you?' Another correct statement from her.

They might have got married so quickly because she was pregnant, but who knows, maybe he'd been thinking of marrying her, anyway?

'Mary, why are you digging up the past?'

'Well, I will stop that soon, too.' She smiled at him sadly.

'What do you mean?'

'I went for an interview for a full-time job today.'

'What?'

'I've played the housewife for a long time. I want something different, now.'

'You have enjoyed other activities apart from being a wife and a mother.'

'Yes, but I arranged my activities to fit in with your life first.'

'What are you talking about?'

'Param, any stupid person can do the housework. I have spent most of the last ten years in the house, not because I love dusting and cleaning pots and pans, but because I love you. I wanted to make our life happy.'

'And you have done so. What has changed, now?'

'I don't think you love me enough anymore, as your wife.'

'Pardon?' He was getting angry.

'Param, do you think that I'm the type of woman who will do the cooking and just be available for you to fuck?'

'What are you talking about?'

'I have given enough of my time to our marriage. Now, I want to be me.' Her tone was firm.

'You have always maintained your freedom. Don't say that for the last ten years you haven't done anything but please me.' He was mad, now.

She stayed silent for a while. Then she said: 'I want to go away for a while.'

Was she saying that she was leaving?

'Go away? What about Meera?'

'As you always said, we can put her in a boarding school.'

This was the beginning of his lonely nights, although he wasn't aware of it at the time.

The day started very early for Banu as she got up to go to the airport. She could tell that there was tension between her brother and sister-in-law. She felt sorry for Mary having to deal with all of Param's family problems, yet she found it difficult to talk to her in a relaxed way. There was the language barrier, and they had a different understanding of most things.

When she got in the car, Meera came and asked, 'Can I come, too, Daddy?'

'Of course.' Param opened the car for his daughter.

'Who is coming from Sri Lanka?' Meera asked him when her father started the car.

'Your uncle, Auntie Banu's friend.'

'Oh. Will he stay with us?'

'Yes, for a while.'

'Mum said we are already very crowded.'

Banu looked at her brother and said, 'We don't want to bring trouble into your life. Let Sabesan stay with his friends until we sort out something.'

'Don't worry about it,' he said. He didn't tell her that Mary was going away for a while.

'Sabesan has to study. He shouldn't neglect his study and work. Besides, we have enough room for all of us.'

'Yes, I know, but I don't want to upset Mary.' Banu sounded sad.

'You're not upsetting anyone.'

'She has been wonderful to me up to now...'
'What's wrong, then?'
'I feel very uncomfortable with this atmosphere.'
'That's not your problem.' He smiled sadly.
'Whatever it is, we shouldn't force our way of life onto Mary.' Banu was an advisor, now?
'You are so sensible to think that way. But Mary's problem is very different.'

They went to the airport terminal. They had to wait for a long time before they saw Sabesan. The immigration officers demanded proof that Sabesan was going to be a student and asked many questions.

'Why do they have to ask so many questions?' Sabesan complained on the way home.

'The British think that third world people have nothing better to do than to come here to conquer their country,' Param said bitterly.

'So, we have to suffer in Sri Lanka because we are Tamils, we have to suffer here because we are black,' Banu told her boyfriend. She looked very happy to see him. She had been worried to death for the last three months.

'Did you tell your family about you and Banu?' Param asked him.

'No, but Karthiga will.'
'Will they be shocked?'
'I have no idea.'
'And you don't care?'
'Not at all.' Sabesan was getting irritated with Param's questions.

Banu was opening the parcels from Sir Lanka.

'This is from my sister to you,' Sabesan gave Banu a parcel. It was a wedding sari.

Banu burst into tears.

'Your sister is a nice woman,' Banu said to Sabesan.

Param's thoughts went to Sri Lanka and to Karthiga for a minute; he knew that he was desperate to see her.

'This is for you, Param.' Sabesan handed another parcel to Meera to open for him.

She opened it. 'It's a book, Daddy.'

A Hindu religious book. *Bhagavad Gita*.

He smiled at the book, as it was from Karthiga, and thought, what is she trying to do? I don't think I'll ever be a saint and release myself from the reality of the world.

# Chapter 14

Param had to tell his mother and his sister in Colombo about Banu and Sabesan. When he phoned his mother and told her that he was organising a wedding for Banu and Sabesan, she was crying as she knew the news already from Mahadeva's family in Jaffna.

'Why do you insult us like this, my son, I wish you had never come to Jaffna for your father's funeral'.

He felt sorry for her. She was living in a past which was controlled by tradition, the caste system and inhuman ideologies.

His sister in Colombo and her husband did not shout at him but said, 'We hope Banu won't think about coming to our home; she is no longer our sister.'

What a cruel thing to say? The Tamils in Jaffna who believe in the caste system will never allow the society to go forward, he thought angrily.

He organised a simple registry wedding in London for Banu and Sabesan.

The house was filled with people who were there for Banu and Sabesan's marriage. Mahadeva was completely drunk and loud. He was shouting and screaming about Banu getting married to a low-caste man. He threatened to divorce Gowry because her sister was marrying a low-caste man. He threatened to organise high-caste Tamil men to beat up Sabesan in London.

Mary just watched them. It was like a life drama; some were acting, some were watching. No one had control of the situation. She didn't know what to do for a while. She wanted to throw Mahadeva out of the house when he started to behave like a thug, but wondered if it were her place to do so.

Gowry was in the corner of the house sobbing. Sabesan was simmering with anger, but Banu took him upstairs.

When Mahadeva started to talk about Karthiga and Param, Param asked him to stop talking nonsense.

Param said, 'I don't like people talking about my personal life.'

'What does this have to do with your personal life?' Mahadeva was drunk and unsteady on his feet.

'Why don't you shut up and get out, you narrow-minded bastard.' Param shouted at him.

'You won't let me talk, will you, but there are lots of people in Colombo talking about you. Do you know what they are saying?' Mahadeva came forward pointing his finger at Param, speaking in Tamil.

'I don't care what others say. You shut up,' Param shouted.

'I will shut up, but I must tell you this.'

Mahadeva switched to English, for Mary's hearing. 'How would you react if I went to Sri Lanka and had a nice time after marrying your sister? But I am not like you, with a wife in England and a girlfriend in Sri Lanka.'

'Please get out,' Param said, breathing heavily.

Mahadeva continued his drunken tirade in English. 'I am going to leave, soon. Who wants to stay in a house with a low-caste bastard and his lot, anyway, but I tell you this, you can shut me up here, but you cannot shut up the people who saw you with Sabesan's sister in the cinema, at the beach, in Galle Road and at her house…' Mahadeva laughed loudly like a madman.

Param couldn't take it, anymore. How could Mahadeva be so vindictive, purposely bringing up the subject to humiliate him in front of others, in front of Mary and Meera?

Param punched Mahadeva so hard that his nose started to bleed. Mahadeva held his nose and walked out screaming, 'I will kill you, I will kill you.'

Gowry ran after her husband. It was pouring with rain outside. Mahadeva was falling across Mary's well-maintained flowerbed, still shouting in English, 'What kind of man are you? Cheating two women, or maybe many women.'

Param ran after him, very angry, but Banu held him back and said, 'Please, my dear brother, ignore him, he is drunk.'

Mary looked at her husband very calmly. 'You see, I wasn't wrong at all. You have changed since you went to Sri Lanka,' she said to him in front of Banu and Sabesan.

Param didn't say a word. He said to Banu, 'It is getting late. The registrar is waiting for us.'

He left the house as Gowry was coming back to the house soaking wet.

'Why don't you follow your drunken husband?' Param demanded.

Banu, Sabesan and Gowry were ready to go to the registry office.

Param waited in the car for Mary, but she didn't come. 'Shall I go and get her?' Banu offered.

'No, let her be alone.' He started his car. Meera came running up: 'Daddy, please take me.' She got into the car.

No one said much in the car for a long time. Mahadeva had destroyed any chance of Param sorting things out, problems which he had hoped he could mend after Banu's wedding.

'I am sorry, Banu, this is your special day. The bastard Mahadeva has done a lot of damage.' Param felt sorry for Banu having to face Mary's anger on her special day.

'Don't worry about us. You need to worry about Mary,' said Banu comfortingly.

'Well, if I had control of my life, I would have changed it to something better,' he said, trying to be philosophical.

'There is no such thing as not being able to control our own lives,' Sabesan started to argue.

'Please stop arguing. Haven't we had enough arguments already?' Gowry snapped at all of them.

'Why didn't you go with your husband?' Param said to Gowry.

'Leave him alone; he was drunk. Besides, in London I have no one except Banu and you.' Gowry said.

'I hope he will forgive you for coming to the wedding.' Param said sarcastically to his sister, but she remained silent.

'Sabesan, if your organisation ever comes to power in the Tamil homeland, how would you deal with people like Mahadeva, who are fanatics on Hindu fundamentalism and on the caste and dowry systems?'

'There are lots of things to be changed in our society, not only caste, class, the dowry system, but also the attitudes about women's position in society as a whole'.

Sabesan hadn't finish his sentence before Gowry interrupted him. 'It's all very well for you to talk about women in Tamil society. How will anything change unless men change themselves? Refusing to get married wouldn't get us anywhere. The social system in Tamil society won't allow a woman to be free from pressure unless she is married.'

'How could you marry a person you'd never met?' Param asked Gowry.

'Living so many years in England has made you ask that question. If you were in Sri Lanka, you might have done the same thing,' Gowry returned the attack.

'I don't think I would have sold myself to a woman I had never met.'

'Brother Param, it's easy for you to say that. Perhaps in western society people fall in love and get married; in our society people get married then fall in love.' Gowry said.

'Do you really believe that?' Param couldn't believe anyone could fall in love with that moron Mahadeva. Poor Gowry.

Not many people were invited to the wedding, but Sabesan's friends, most of them politically active Tamil youths, had organised a reception. They talked about Tamil Eelam (homeland, a separate country for Tamils in Sri Lanka) and their struggle to achieve it. They all gave their congratulations to Param for helping two people of different castes marry. Param was so happy to see Sabesan and Banu together and wished Karthiga were there to see it.

He would write to her tonight and tell her how happy he was that her fear for Sabesan's life in Sri Lanka was over, now. Sabesan could study in England while Banu worked earning money to help him.

Param had booked a hotel in Kent for their honeymoon, Sabesan mumbling something about spending lots of money. Param laughed and said, 'A honeymoon doesn't come often. Enjoy yourself.'

He drove them to the Kent countryside. He then took Gowry to her new house in Wimbledon, telling her she could come back home with him if she was scared to go home alone to Mahadeva.

'If you have to cross the water to get to the other side, you cannot wait for a bridge to be built. You have to use whatever you can to get to the other side. Marriage is really the same. If you want to live with somebody you have to work very hard to build a relationship strong enough to get through the marriage. This is my fate to live with Mahadeva. I can't run away from it.' Gowry sounded like a philosopher.

'It's easy to duck the issue, to put the blame on fate and God, isn't it? Why don't you fight for yourself rather than go along with what he says?' Param said.

'Building a bridge isn't as easy as breaking. Relationships are always a complicated matter. Let me handle my own life.' Gowry said firmly.

He kept himself quiet after that.

When they arrived at Gowry's house Param went in with her. They both went upstairs and found Mahadeva lying on the settee in the front room. Gowry washed his face with cold water to wake him up.

Param stared, watching his sister nurse her drunken husband. Would she have to do it often? he wondered.

When Mahadeva came to his senses, he started to shout at Param. 'Who invited in this bastard who is fucking a low caste?'

Before Param could reply, his sister said, 'Don't start anything. Please go home.' Gowry led her brother downstairs.

Param got into the car, and he sat watching his sister's house for a few minutes. He could hear Mahadeva screaming at Gowry about bringing Param into his house. He felt so sorry for his sister having to be married to this stupid, arrogant and narrow-minded man.

Meera was fast asleep in the back of the car, as he started the car and headed home.

Thinking of Mary, he realised that as soon as he got home, he would have to do some explaining about Mahadeva's remarks concerning his stay in Sri Lanka. He wished he had explained it to her a long time ago. He didn't want Meera growing up in a tense atmosphere. His responsibility was nearly completed, now. He had no more sisters to worry about. Gowry was married to a moron, alright, but she was settled, and Banu would be fine with Sabesan.

Param needed to talk to Mary about lots of things about his past, the main subject being Karthiga. He needed to tell Mary everything.

He stopped the car and looked at his house. Usually, there was a light on in front of the house, but tonight it was all dark. He carried Meera to the door and rang the bell, as he found it difficult to open the door with Meera on his shoulder. There was no sign of anyone. He struggled to open the door and put the lights on.

'Mary,' he called.

He went upstairs and put Meera on her bed then went into his bedroom and turned the light on. He could immediately sense that something was missing.

There was a letter on the blue bed cover, like a boat sailing on the sea.

He could feel butterflies in his stomach. His pulse was beating faster as he opened the letter.

'Param, I am leaving you…'

He lay on the bed, with a lump in his throat, and stared at the empty white ceiling.

'Mary, please come back.' He called to her as if she were outside the door. 'I will explain everything. Please, please give me a chance.'

He started to read the letter.

It was a letter of a few pages. Finishing a marriage of over ten years with an explanation of a few pages. Her suspicions, raised because of Param's mood and behaviour since returning from Sri Lanka, had been confirmed by Mahadeva's remarks about Param and Sabesan's sister, she said in the letter.

'You could have been more honest with me,' she accused him. 'I don't believe in living together for the sake of children, society or status unless two people love and are honest to each other. I don't think we have that close a relationship anymore, certainly not close enough to stay married.

'I can understand your feelings for your former girlfriend in Ceylon, and I remember that you wanted to go back home as soon as you finished your study. My pregnancy stopped you from going. You are a man with principles, such as not wanting to upset the people who love you. You told me you came to London because your father wanted you to do further study. I knew we weren't lovers but good friends, and we made a mistake sleeping together.

'You married me because of Meera, but I know you loved us very much. But that loving Param got lost somewhere in Sri Lanka. I have no idea what exactly what do you expected me to do. But I am not prepared to live with you just because we have a daughter to care for. I know you love Meera more than anything in the world.

'I want you to be happy. But I do not think you have the same feeling towards me anymore. I don't want Meera to grow up in an emotionally artificial environment. I want her to understand things as they are. She is a bright girl. She will understand. I will have permission to see her and have her any time I want.

'As I said before, I don't want to be a full-time mother, anymore. You can put her in boarding school, and we will have her in the holidays. I am very upset and will be staying with a friend in Scotland for a while. Then I will start my new job and start a new life. I will wish you all the best. Thank you for a life that was beautiful until you went to Sri Lanka.—Mary.'

Mary was gone.

He felt the emptiness and the pain so sharply. He wanted to have a happy home.

But where is my home? What is home without a family? How will I explain things to Meera? He wanted to scream. He felt tense, angry and most of all, lonely.

His love for Karthiga was based on romantic love. Had his love for Mary begun based mainly on his loneliness in London? Mary's friendship and love had made him love London. Mary determined to take Param to her father, who was not happy with the match, but Mary made her father to change his mind about Param, seeing Param's dedication to their marriage.

Mary's father, with his ancestry in the British colonial administration, felt proud to rule half the planet. But her mother was kind to Param. She adored her only granddaughter, Meera. They loved that their only daughter Mary had found a decent man as her husband.

What would Param do, now? As Mary told him, he would have to find a boarding school for Meera. Soon Sabesan and Banu would find a place of their own and go away.

What am I going to do? Grow old alone? He looked at the clock. It was two-thirty in the morning. The whole world was fast asleep except him. No one to share his life with his feelings. He thought, I must pull myself together and do something, now.

He dialled the number.

She answered.

'Hello, Liz?'

'Who is it?' She seemed very sleepy.

'Me.'

'Me, who?'

'Param.'

'Param? What's the matter?'

'Can I talk to you?'

'Of course, but not now, please.' She put the phone down.

Autumn came sooner than he expected. There was so much wind that it had blown all the leaves away, leaving the trees naked and as sad-looking as his mind at the time. He found a boarding school for Meera not far from London as he wanted her to come home at the weekends. His little girl was so upset to go away to a private school. She said she wanted to be at home with Daddy.

'You will get used to the new place and find some lovely friends, soon, my darling.' He kissed his daughter when he left her. His heart ached, his mind was confused, he felt an incredible pain and sadness when he walked away.

After that, he had seen Mary only a few times during the last two months. Meera had always been closer to Param than Mary. For her, Banu had nearly taken the place of her mother. Meera loved her Aunt Banu and Uncle Sabes.

Param brought Liz home a few times to see Meera. Liz was very motherly towards Meera, which made the situation easier than Param had thought it would be, being without Mary. Banu couldn't understand her brother bringing another woman into the house as soon as Mary left home. Banu was confused about the way of life in London. Too many people, too much complexity to deal with.

Param did not wanted to upset Banu or Sabesan by telling them that his relationship with Mary had broken down due to his visit to Sri Lanka. What else could he have done, with family who were in need. Could he have left his loving sister Banu to stay in Sri Lanka to see the man loves killed by the Sri Lankan forces? He did that to please Karthiga. Bringing Sabesan to London, he hoped, also helped her old father and mentally vulnerable mother.

Param was confused, as things were changing rapidly around his life. All his life he'd tried to do his duty for his family. That didn't seem to be working as he'd expected, as he couldn't please everyone.

# Chapter 15

After Mary left, Banu ran the house for Sabesan and Param. He felt more like a lodger in his own home.

He wrote many times to Karthiga after Mary left him. He didn't tell her that Mary left him because Mahadeva had told Mary about Karthiga and him. But he told her that Mary was not happy with him at the moment and was staying in Scotland because of her job; but he knew that someone must have written to her and told her that he was without a wife, now.

He suffered the pain of being alone in his room. He would wake up in the middle of the night reaching out to embrace Mary like he used to, and then realise that it wouldn't happen again. The cold autumn weather and his loneliness made him look for a partner to go out to plays or the cinema with.

All his life, he managed his life with his knowledge, experience, and the unexpected changes which made him to make some unavoidable decisions. He could find the answer to his question of: what's happening to me all of a sudden, did I get trapped in this situation consciously or unconsciously? He considered that most of the time, he acted accordingly to the judgements of his inner thoughts. This situation was much more painful than anything he'd ever experienced in his life.

He was lucky that Liz was in London. She'd been with him when he was travelling with his mind in turmoil about seeing the family in Sri Lanka. She comforted him on the Colombo beach, when Sabesan told him about Karthiga's barbaric experience. He met her at Victoria station when his relationship with Mary was breaking up. Liz was a person who cares about people with no expectation of anything in return.

He felt that every time he was in need of moral support, she was there to ease his mind. Was it a coincidence or for some other reason? He was not one to analyse things, now; he wanted to go along with them. He did not want to complicate anything more at the moment. He wanted Liz' friendship.

He spent more time out with Liz than at home with Banu, Sabesan and Meera.

'Thank God, I met you on the plane,' he said to Liz when they were coming out of a cinema one night.

'Well, if not me, you would have found someone else. Men don't feel happy unless they have a woman with them,' she told him.

She may have been right.

'I do not know how to cope with my situation; it seems like I am walking through a dark tunnel at times.'

'Param, life is not like walking through a summer garden or having a summer vacation in an exotic place like Sri Lanka. Life has its own rhythm with all four seasons. We have to learn to live through the cold winter, have a smile when we see a sign of bright light and gentle warmth and to see a daffodil. We love the spring to appreciate the wonder of nature. Inhale the fragrance of loving flowers in the summer as we are in a sort of a magical world. The autumn comes, we see the reality of our existence as gloomy, windy, and cold, and we fear for heavy snow and difficulties.'

He just looked at her. Had she come across painful situations in her life? he asked himself.

'Enjoy every minute of it, if possible, and live through with the determination to survive and face the challenges, that's my principle,' Liz said with her loving smile.

Param instructed Sabesan and Banu not to write anything about his family affairs to Karthiga, but he always suspected Mahadeva of stirring up trouble between people.

'How long will I have to hide the truth from Karthiga?' He told her in one of his letters of his intention to visit Sri Lanka soon and how much he was longing to see her. She wrote to thank him for helping Sabesan, but after that she stopped writing.

Sathyan wrote saying that he had visited Karthiga few times, and she had taken an interest in politics. 'You see, if all the men in the world expected that women could do more than men currently think them capable of, they can do wonders,' he wrote.

Liz was getting ready to go to India, again. Last year she hadn't managed to complete her journey because of her sister's suicide attempt.

Param liked to spend time with Liz, and she was aware of this. She was trying to help him to get through this bad patch in his life. Liz also knew that Param was trying very hard to fill his life with someone else. She liked him, and found him very open, and more like a child at times, in need of someone to comfort him. He was unhappy about his life; she knew that.

Liz understood his fear of being alone in London. He was not so westernised that he could find a casual partner to enjoy life with. He wouldn't get involved with someone unless he understood them and felt easy being with them.

Param phoned Liz often, now, and she was becoming more and more involved in his life. Even though she was sometimes busy at work, he would make her come with him to the cinema, a play, or for a walk. Sometimes she complained that he expected too much from her, and that she could not give so much time to him.

'Don't think I will replace Karthiga or Mary in your life, but I do want you to be happy,' she told him openly.

'I never expected that from you. I just want you to be my friend, not a lover,' he said.

'But friendship can lead onto something else, too,' she warned him.

'I know.' He drank his glass of wine, studying her face.

He respected Liz very much. She was a talented woman, as well as a beautiful personality. Every time they met, he felt more deeply toward her and wanted to see more of her. She was interested in so many things, from western classical music to Ravi Shankar's guitar music.

'Haven't you got a boyfriend?' he asked her once.

'No,' she smiled.

'A girlfriend?'

'No,' she laughed.

'Aren't you human?' he teased her.

'Are you asking whether I have someone to make love with? I don't have a lover, now, but I have lots of friends. I am nearly thirty. I don't want to waste time on romance and the illusion of love. I need a lover to make love, like any normal person. I finished a relationship about two years ago. Partly, that was the reason for my journey to India, to forget the past. Since then, lots of things have happened, and I am busy doing my writing and other things, and now I am friendly with you. It doesn't mean that we should hop into bed just because we are both lonely.'

'Why not?' he finally brought up the subject. 'Is there anything wrong with making love to a person you like? What is the matter with that?' he asked her.

Liz would not answer. She knew that he was drunk. She got up and they started walking. He felt uncomfortable putting out the question of about making love. He wanted her to feel happy when she was with him. She would not go further to talk about the subject.

They went to see a Shyam Bengal film. Liz was madly in love with an Indian actress Smita Patil and her acting. They walked along the Thames after the film, near County Hall. It was about eleven o'clock at night. There were leisure boats carrying drunken party goers along the river. The Parliament buildings stood in front of them on the other side of the river like imperialistic symbols.

He put his arm around her and turned her face towards him.

He had held Karthiga exactly like that, on Colombo beach. He'd held Mary many years ago in the same spot, and now Liz. He felt all three women just next to each other in front of him. He let Liz move away and sat on the steps going down to the Thames, watching the waves touching the steps.

'Are you thinking about Karthiga?' Liz asked him. She was standing at the top of the steps. He turned back and stared at her, but he couldn't see the expression on her face. He didn't answer her question.

'Do you still love her?'

He didn't answer. He sat there without saying a word. She came and sat very close to him.

'My pride wouldn't allow me to let myself be used by you,' she said calmly.

'Used by me?'

'Sorry if I have used the phrase inappropriately, what I am saying is I don't want you to try and put me in the place of Karthiga or Mary.'

'Oh Liz, please don't say that. You are different. Why do you say such silly things?'

'I am not being silly. I don't want to lose my identity and become your...'

'Why do you talk about being mine? I'm not intending to control anyone.'

'Yes, you are.'

'What?'

'You are still emotionally controlling Karthiga by thinking of her and doing things for her. You will have some involvement with Mary because of the child you have in common. Am I meant to fill the rest of your needs?'

'What do you mean?'

'Sharing a bed with you for the sake of sex?'

He stood up and buttoned his jacket angrily, 'Please try to understand me. If you think I am only friendly with you because I want to sleep with you, then I won't see you again.' He was cross.

She gently put her arm around him and kissed him. It was a beautiful moment, he thought.

'Param, you know perfectly well that I like you very much and say truly what I feel about you. But please do not rush into things for the sake of feeling loved and wanted. Let life pass by you, but do not try hard to change it to please your feelings. Allow yourself to get healed from the hurts. The summer will come soon, you may feel better, then,' Liz said lovingly.

They stayed silent together for a long time. The night was slightly cold, but the stars in the sky were brilliant.

'Param, you fell in love with Karthiga when you were in your late teens; that's a romance as pure and deep as any one's first love. And you left her to come to London to please your father, then you married to Mary when you were in your mid-twenties because of Meera. All these things were without much control on your part, and you did not have much time to think and act upon your thoughts. Now, you and I are not under any pressure to commit to anything under present circumstances.' She carefully expressed her thoughts so as not to hurt his feelings.

He stayed quiet, resting his head on her shoulder as she had done on their flight to Russia. They felt easy with each other. Understood each other.

'Param, I want to think things over. I will be away for a while. If you can rid yourself of your guilty conscience over Karthiga, if you can sort things out with Mary, please do that. You said you were going to explain to Mary about Karthiga, but she left before your explanation. She felt you were living with her, having a child with her and all, but you never really allowed yourself to be honest to her.' It sounded to him as if Liz really wanted him to go back to his life with Mary.

'Liz, I never wanted to hide anything from Mary, but when we got together, she was the one who told me not to talk about the past.' He never meant to be dishonest to Mary.

'Maybe Mary had a past which she never wanted think back on and feel sad or bad about, but you did not write to Karthiga when you married Mary. Why?' Liz was cross examining him about his past? He looked at her questioningly.

'It was too much for me to suddenly realise that I was going to be a father, then we had to get married. I did not want Mary's parents to feel that I had taken advantage of their daughter, who was so kind to me and saved my life from the racist thugs. Most of all, I would never have allowed an abortion of my child inside her…' He was upset that he had to bring up the confusing and painful past to justify his present situation.

'Param, I know you wouldn't take an advantage of a woman who trusted you. When we were in Russia you were lovely and friendly but never went over the line, although I did not know that time you were a married man.'

He did not say anything as she was not completely right about him, but she has had some kind of instinct to understand people much better than others. He knew any man will fall in love with her because of her fantastic manner, her knowledge of reality and her feminine beauty.

She understood his silence and said, 'When I come back, we can talk things over. You know perfectly well that I like you and I want you to be happy.'

Christmas was coming soon and snow was falling. The holidaymakers who were trying to get away for the winter were packed up at the airport. Liz sat near him without a word. The weather had been just like this when he came with Mary to the airport last year to go to Sri Lanka.

Now, Liz was going to India. Because of the bad weather, the plane was going to be delayed. 'I hope the weather will be better in India,' Liz said.

'It will be hot, you will have a lovely summer vacation, there,' Param said jokingly, but suddenly he remembered his daughter's words last year, commanding him to 'have a lovely summer vacation, Daddy'.

What was the journey to Sri Lanka for him? A sharp pain went through his thoughts. What a summer it was, he thought.

They both wandered around for a while. How many Tamils would see them together, now? Mahadeva could write another letter home. Who cares?

Param had received a solicitor's letter already from Mary, who was filing for a divorce on the grounds of adultery.

'Adultery with whom?' He wanted to laugh.

Love, marriage, all simply destroyed in one solicitor's letter. He left the letter on the table when he left for the airport with Liz. Love was a strange matter, it had the power of manipulating human nature without the consent of the people involved.

He didn't know whether he loved Liz, Karthiga or Mary or not one of them, but he wanted to be with Liz until she left London. He didn't even know whether he was capable of really loving anyone, now. With Liz, he just wanted to continue as they were.

She wept when she left him. 'Please try to be happy,' she told him.

'I wish you weren't going away,' he kissed her tenderly.

'Don't expect someone else to sort out your problems. I couldn't help you even if I were staying in London at present, as you have so much in your plate. Try to be independent,' she advised him.

Someone else? Liz was not just someone else to him. He noticed her blonde hair spread across her shoulders as she held him tight.

She boarded, and the plane took off in the middle of thick fog and heavy snow.

He opened the door for her. He hadn't seen Mary for three months. She had come to collect Meera for the Christmas holidays. She came with a very handsome white man, who she introduced to Param as her 'boyfriend'.

Param shook hands with Mary's boyfriend and, despite the shock, said 'hello',

telling him how nice it was to meet him.

Mary wouldn't look Param in the eye. Most of the time she was there, they were never alone at all. She asked him whether he was going to sell the house, and he said he would settle that matter, soon.

Banu and Sabesan weren't there when she came. She told him to give her love to Banu.

'You seem happy,' he said, trying to be friendly.

'Yes, I found real love,' she snapped at him.

'Well, good luck,' he wished her sincerely, his voice was soft, but his mind was cracking into pieces.

Sabesan spent quite a lot of time with people in London who advocated armed struggle for Tamils in Sri Lanka. And after Liz left, Param stayed indoors a lot and discussed Tamil politics with them. Param had never liked the idea of armed struggle; it was not that he didn't support freedom for the Tamil people, but he believed that Tamil organisations didn't yet have constructive strategies.

'So, who will help you all in this armed struggle?' Param questioned Sabesan.

'India, of course.' Sathyan said.

'Why should India get involved in Sri Lankan internal politics?'

'Because it is a neighbouring country as well as a country which has about fifty million Tamils living in it. India has to help the Tamil struggle.'

'That is rubbish. India has its own problems of internal uncertainty, why should they get involved in Sri Lanka?' Param certainly didn't agree with any country getting involved with another country's politics. He hated American involvement in Latin America and Russian involvement in Afghanistan.

'India has no choice but to get involved,' Sabesan's vision looked far ahead.

'So, you don't care if our country is dominated by another country?' Param asked.

'That's the Sri Lankan government's fault, by not solving the Tamil issue.

Tamils are not going to suffer any longer. We have to fight for our rights.'

'Don't you ever consider that your emotional ideas might destroy a nation?'

'What do you mean?' Sabesan got angry.

'We, the Tamils, will not be able to organise a big military force to beat a Sri Lankan army. I will never believe that India would support separatism, so in the long run our people are going to suffer more than you can ever imagine.'

'Yes, yes, you are all scared to fight, you just run away for a better life. There are people who have nothing to lose but stand to gain freedom if they fight.' Sabesan raised his voice.

'Yes, I believe that, but I don't think we should rely on India for aid.' Param tried to control his anger.

'What else can we do?'

Sabesan's question irritated Param. 'Rely on our own people. Identify our enemies. Don't ever let Indian soldiers come to our land and take our women.' Param said firmly.

Sabesan had to work hard to save money to pay his fees. The British government had put the fees up for foreign students, in order to encourage white working-class people to attend college rather than allowing rich foreign students to come and fill all the places.

But Sabesan was in no way rich. He worked day and night to save money. One day he was attacked by National Front thugs on the way home from night work and was quite badly beaten up. He had to have stitches for a broken nose.

Gowry and Mahadeva came to see him, but Param didn't like Mahadeva being there at all. It was all because of Mahadeva that Param's life was in a mess, he thought.

'Where can we go and live in peace?' Sabesan moaned.

'There is no place on earth without problems. We have to learn to live with the situation in which we find ourselves,' said Param.

'Yes, otherwise, people run away from us.' Mahadeva's stupid remarks made everybody angry.

Param had received a letter from Sathyan from Colombo saying that Sinhalese soldiers had been on the rampage in Jaffna town. Many thousands of pounds worth of property was burned, and many people had been killed. Hundreds of Tamil youths had been arrested under suspicion of terrorist activities.

'I want to go home and fight, I don't want to stay here and suffer dirty treatment by white thugs for the sake of a few luxuries,' Sabesan said.

'What?' Param nearly screamed, hearing this. He had thought that Sabesan would give up politics and settle into a life with Banu in London. But now he was saying that he wanted to go home?

Banu said that he should think about his sisters and their future.

Sabesan said, 'If everyone thought about their own lives, who would work for our nation? I love you, Banu, and I love my sisters, too, and I have been through so much, already. But I am not going to spend all my life working on the factory floor in England, or baking bread in a bakery, for just enough to live on when my people's lives are in the hands of Sinhalese fascists.'

Sabesan spoke with emotion and with strong political conviction. Faced with unspeakable oppression, was there really a difference between politics and emotions?

Param didn't say anything.

Banu wrote to Karthiga explaining Sabesan's decision to go back home. She was undecided herself, whether to go back with her husband or stay in London and study.

'Make up your mind on your own. Don't let anyone influence you,' Param advised.

Banu said, 'I thought he would say something like that. He doesn't know how to live.'

Whatever political differences he had with Sabesan, Param had great respect for his determination to fight for the Tamil cause. Param's worry concerned the politics on which he based that struggle. Every struggle has its nationalists, socialists and fascists.

Sabesan was definitely a progressive minded man, but would his organisation take the socialist or the nationalist path? Didn't he know the Tamil community was traditional and conservative, and that he would have to work very hard to convince them of the need for equality for everyone?

Mary had wanted to sell the house as soon as possible, as she wanted to use the money to buy a house in the Midlands. She and Meera were staying with her cousin in Birmingham for the Christmas holidays. He told her that he would put the house on the market after Christmas.

Liz wrote from India. She loved India—the people, the religions, customs, colourful cloths, she loved them all. But she hated the caste system and the inhumane treatment of minorities. But she didn't mention anything about her personal feelings, whether she was missing him; maybe she had decided it was only a friendship and nothing more than that.

Liz had said that Param was not free in his mind from Karthiga nor Mary, and he knew that he would not be free for a long time. He replied to her, telling her about events in Sri Lanka and Sabesan's decision to go back home. He wrote about Karthiga, saying that she would be disappointed to see Sabesan come back, as she was afraid he would get into trouble as soon as he got to Sri Lanka.

Sabesan may be right. Param had run away from home and the struggle in order to live a comfortable life. But did he really have a comfortable life? Was there any purpose in his life other than simply existing? As Liz put it, Param wanted to live with someone instead of live for someone.

Mary had gone because she didn't think Param was free in his mind to really love her. How about Karthiga? Why wouldn't she write to him? Wouldn't she understand that all this happened because of his love for her?

Banu and Sabesan had moved in with Sabesan's friend just before Christmas, so Param had no one in the house to talk to. He hadn't wanted them to go, especially before Christmas. He felt he couldn't face spending Christmas alone, but he had been too proud to ask them to stay.

Well, he thought, if I'm going to have to learn to live on my own, I'd better start now.

On Christmas Eve he came home from his office party very late. Last year this time he was in Moscow with a beautiful lady next to him on the Russian flight. Now, the house felt empty and sad. He couldn't stand it, but at the same time he didn't want to go anywhere else to kill his loneliness. He was determined to be alone and to face it.

On Christmas day, he got up and made himself a cup of coffee. The house was full of cooking smells from next door, turkey and other goodies.

He went for a ride to Hampstead Heath. It was a cold morning, but the sun was shining. He walked slowly in the woods and sat on a bench on Parliament Hill and thought about his life. Life is a jungle, no one knowing what to expect next. Sometimes you hear a bird singing, other times you hear a tiger roar.

Param looked down on London from the Parliament Hill.

All those houses have husbands, wives, children or lovers, or even friends. Who will I have when I go home in Islington, only few miles away from here? I am in my mid-thirties. I don't want to spend the rest of my life alone, he told himself.

He walked back to the woods, remembering walking with Karthiga in Victoria Park in Colombo. Will I ever forget her? And why should I forget her? She's single; my wife will divorce me soon, then I will be single. I must write to her and ask her whether she will take me back.

He stayed until midday in the park, thinking things over. 'Would Liz say I was replacing Mary with Karthiga, just to have someone to look after my daughter? No, she wouldn't think that way.

He came home determined to write to Karthiga. He didn't want to hurry. He must write very carefully. He went over the words in his mind whilst he was cooking himself fried egg on toast for his Christmas lunch, and after lunch he sat at the table to write.

He explained his love for her and how he had got involved with Mary. Although he had started to write very carefully, after a few pages he began to let his feelings overflow. He wrote that he should not have listened to his father about his future and should have married Karthiga and stayed in Ceylon. Now, he had no future, and he could not live without her love. He wrote a very long letter. After that, he slept peacefully.

On Boxing Day, he went to see Banu and Sabesan to see how they were getting on in their new home. Sabesan's friend, who had gone to Nigeria to work, was letting them stay in his house for a while. Banu looked busy and seemed happy to have a place of their own.

'You should come here for your meals,' Banu told her brother.

Was she is taking the place of his mother to care for him, now? he thought.

He stroked her hair lovingly and said confidently, 'Thank you, my little sister, but no, I want to learn to cook for myself.'

He felt that Banu was going to say something, but she was reluctant to continue.

'What is the matter?' he asked her.

'Do you think our father put a curse on you or something, as he did not want you to marry Karthiga or Mary?'

He put his hand on her mouth to stop her talking further. 'I do not believe in mumbo jumbo,' he smiled firmly.

He stayed for a meal with them. He wanted to talk to them of his decision regarding Karthiga, but he couldn't. The letter which he had written was not yet posted.

The next day he went for a long walk in the morning around the Canonbury Canal. Came home to the empty house. Talked to Meera on the phone; he was missing his darling daughter so much. The loneliness was unbearable.

Back to work after few days, and he felt better seeing known faces in the office. After the Christmas holiday, the streets were quite busy. Last year this time he was in Tbilisi in Georgia, not knowing when the flight would leave and worried about his father and his family in London. At that time he never thought how life would turn into a mess.

He posted the letter to Karthiga.

He walked around Upper Street which was full of people busy with the post-Christmas sales. He bought a few presents for Meera. He went home to find lots of letters and Christmas and New Year cards.

There was a letter. In Karthiga's handwriting.

His pulse rate started to rise. She hadn't written to him since finding out about Mary leaving him. He sat on the chair making himself comfortable and opened the letter; he kissed the letter as he wanted to kiss Karthiga.

Then as he read through the letter his heart started to break piece by piece.

'My dear Param, you said that until I got married you wouldn't be happy, my dearest, all my life I prayed for your happiness. I want you to be happy. So, I am getting married. Not because you requested it, but because I think I fell in love with Sathyan. I hope you will go back to your wife and be happy. Sathyan is wonderful, otherwise, who else would marry a woman with such a rotten past? I will be a good wife to him. He says he is very happy, too. I have told him about you. I have nothing to hide from my husband. I want him to understand me, and he loves me enough to go through a long life with me. I hope you will give us your blessing for our future, and we will wish you the best for your happiness with your family forever. It may take some time to understand the sudden changes in our lives. Please forgive me if I had upset you while you were in Sri Lanka. As I know that you are trying to please many people, but please take care of yourself. I will pray for you and your family's happiness.

She signed it: 'Karthiga Sathyan'.

He closed his eyes, tears flowing down his cheeks like a river. He was alone, and cried for hours, he didn't know whether he was crying with sadness for his lost love or with happiness that Karthiga was getting married to Sathyan and was happy. He did know that he was stupid for not telling Mary, regardless of her insistence on not talking about the past. He'd wanted to tell her about his meeting with Karthiga in Colombo, but the course of events gave him no opportunity to explain anything.

Now, he was reading Karthiga's letter about her marriage. He wanted to be happy for her. He praised Sathyan and wished them both every happiness. He poured a glass of whisky and raised the glass in the air saying,

'Cheers, Karthiga Sathyan.' He poured more and more. He felt happy. Very happy, completely drunk and out his mind.

Then the telephone rang. 'You should have collected Meera, today. Remember, I told you Peter and I are going to Paris tomorrow evening for New Year?' Mary said angrily and put down the phone. He promised to come in the morning.

His head was aching, and his eyes were hurt. He hadn't slept at all last night.

The motorway was completely congested with cars. Maybe they were all going to collect their children from their separated mothers or fathers in order to let them go off with their lovers to Paris for New Year.

This time last year, he was going to Jaffna by train with his sister's family to do his last duty for his father. Did my father put a curse on me as Banu said? Now, I have no Karthiga or Mary. His mind was filled with too many questions.

Now, he only had the treasure of his life that was his beautiful daughter Meera. Also he could count on the relationship of his special friend Liz who had been there in Russia and Sri Lanka and in London to comfort him when he faced the challenges of life.

He had two sisters in London. The sisters needed his help and love. But he was alone in his life, with no one to love and to share his passion and sex. He was in a world of darkness.

But his wife Mary, former girl-friend Karthiga and his 'special friend' Liz, all wanted him to be happy.

How can I be happy? he asked himself. His thoughts were going to and fro, analysing the losses and gains of his past. He wanted to be assertive and think carefully about the situation which was unbearably painful.

Respecting the complexity of the present events, he said to himself that he must not be drawn into inappropriate action. He was secure in his home, but he seemed to be a different man with a restless mind and fear of tomorrow and his future.

He remembered what Liz said to him, 'Do not think of the past often, particularly if it disturbs your peace and stability in life. Do not think about your future a lot, either, as the future is too unpredictable, and most of the time, we have to face challenges which may be dependent on the strength of our minds. Please, my dearest Param, just work on the issue of the present. That's your duty, and use your knowledge and experience to tackle it'.

He spoke out loud, as if Liz were next to him and listening to him. 'Yes, my present existence is being with my darling daughter, who has the power to stir my inner feelings for the betterment of both of our lives. I must control my mind, overcome this fear of being alone, as I have a daughter who needs me. If I do not get there on time to collect her, Mary may take her with them to Paris. I will not let her take my daughter from me.'

He had a sudden urge to be with Meera immediately, he could not waste a minute without someone to love him and be close to him. He was not alone; he had the most beautiful daughter, a beautiful young lady who was giving him unlimited love; he was not alone. He told himself to be firm and strong. He 'would fight any challenge' and 'live only for her', he promised himself.

He put his foot down hard on the accelerator. The speedometer was going up and up.

He saw the dim lights from the highway like a dream. In the dream he saw Karthiga's face, her tears, the reflection of lights in her tears, Mary's angry face, Liz's happy face, most of all his daughter's face, filled with sadness of not to being with Daddy, now. The images came and went, on and on; he couldn't stop seeing them; he wanted to run away faster and faster.

He lost control. The car hit the hard shoulder and something else. Some time later, there were police and ambulance sirens filling the air. Param, who had responded to circumstances which put him through unbearable tests, did not obey the inner voice saying, 'do not speed'.

This Param, the man who was now head of the family, the man who was so determined to fulfil his duty, lost his mind for a few seconds from being alone in the world with no one to love him. He suddenly saw just an empty dark tunnel in front of him. No Mary to there to rescue him with love, no Meera to run to him, no Karthiga or Liz always wanting him to be happy.

It took them a long time to free Param's injured, bloody body from the damaged car. As they looked amongst his belongings, whom would they call, Mary or Banu to identify this unconscious foreign man on the British motorway?

END.

# Acknowledgements

I would like to thank my ex-husband the late Mr. Balasubramaniam who encouraged me to write this novel in Tamil, Mr. A. Jesurasa (Editor of 'Alai' magazine in Jaffna) for publishing the Tamil edition, Ms. Nirmala Rajasingam for writing the foreword and Mr. Pathmanaba Iyer, who introduced me to the Indian-Tamil literary world.

My grateful thanks to my long-time friend Jane Drinkwater for reading the first draft of my translation of this novel, to my dear friend Mary Gilford for doing the first editing, to Susie Helme for her constant support and the final editing and to Elaine Graham-Leigh for her encouragement and proof reading. My sincere thanks also go to the late Mr. K Palanisamy (Kovai Gnani) for encouraging me to translate my Tamil novel into English.

My special thanks to my darling sons, Nirmalan, Arunan and Seran for not disturbing my writing.

I dedicate this novel to the progressive young Tamil men who fought against the caste, class, dowry and religious system and state terrorism in Sri Lanka from 1960-1980 and inspired me to write this novel.